THIEF IN THE NIGHT

JAY .H. DEE

This is a work of fiction. The places, characters, incidents and dialogues are products of the author's imagination and are not to be construed as real. Any resemblance to actual places, events or persons, living or dead, is entirely coincidental.

Scriptures were taken from the King James Version. Public Domain.

Cover Photos by Dave Marr, Jo Verhoef, Lakov Kalinin (courtesy of Deposit Photos), and Jay .H. Dee.
Cover design by Jay .H. Dee, Victoria, Australia.

Thief In The Night

ISBN 978-0-9942436-2-1

NAVY TERMINOLOGY

XO: Executive Officer.

The Bosun or boatswain: is an officer on a ship who is responsible for the rigging, anchors, cables, sails, and other errata that are used to keep a ship running smoothly. He or she is considered to be the foreman of the ship's crew, because this sailor issues orders to the deck crew.

The Coxswain: in the Navy, this is the driver of a small boat, and the senior petty officer on a small ship.

RHIB: Rigid-hulled Inflatable Boat. Each RHIB is 7.2-metres in length and is water jet propelled. Each RHIB is stored in a dedicated cradle and davit, and is capable of operating independently from the patrol boat as they carry their own communications, navigation, and safety equipment.

Crane: This lowers and lifts the RHIBs in and out of the water, from and into their cradle and davit.

Quarter deck: This is the deck space at the rear of the ship.

Bridge: The command centre in the ship.

Galley: The kitchen on board the boat.

Wardroom: a commissioned officers' mess (eating area) on board a warship.

Radar: a system for detecting the presence, direction, distance, and speed of aircraft, ships, and other objects, by sending out pulses of radio waves which are reflected off the object back to the source.

EOD: Electrical Optical Device. This is used to view objects at long range.

Dedicated to the
service men and women
of Australia.
Your labour and your sacrifice
are greatly appreciated.

ACKNOWLEDGEMENTS

Many thanks to my family and friends for their encouragement and for their time in reading this book. Especially thanks to Aunty Jill, Kate and my mum, who were great supporters in this endeavour. Your help and input has been most valuable.

Thanks also to Mary Hawkins for her expertise as an author. I appreciate the time taken to provide extremely helpful writing tips and suggestions for improvement.

Most of all, thanks to God for the inspiration, ideas and collaboration in the writing process. As always, it was a pure delight!

PROLOGUE

New Year's Eve:

A strong hand grasped the sixteen year old boy's arm, twisted it behind his back and rammed him up against the tiled wall. In a mixture of panic and confusion, he could not speak let alone scream. An instant later a syringe was plunged into the arm behind his back and a strange sensation overcame him. Euphoria and fear. Loss of strength in his arms and legs caused him to become limp.

His mind reeled in terror as he was tossed over his attacker's bulky shoulder and carried from the restroom through back passageways of the expensive resort. He wanted to fight, to scream, but was incapable of both. He was paralysed and helpless. His awareness of his surroundings melded into a nightmarish state, hovering between reality and a drug induced hallucination.

He wanted to run back to the resort for protection. Instead he was tossed like a sack of potatoes into the boot of a car, which drove away into the night.

1

"What do you mean your son has been kidnapped?" the police officer fired back in surprise.

Ezekiel Hunter was resplendent in his white tuxedo. It contrasted his short dark hair, which was peppered with grey. His piercing blue eyes bored into the native policeman. "We were at the resort restaurant-"

"Which resort?"

Ezekiel's tone became clipped. "The Southern Star. Rylie went to the restroom and never returned. I went to check on him after fifteen minutes but he wasn't there."

His wife Elizabeth stood at his side, her long slim fingers gripping his arm like a vice. Her mascara had run down her timelessly beautiful face.

The officer's scepticism was almost tangible. "Are you sure he hasn't just snuck out for a night on the town? Such instances are not unusual on Pearl Island."

The grouping of islands, the largest of which was Pearl, were a well known tropical destination not far off the Australian coast. It made its living primarily from tourism.

Ezekiel was growing impatient. "No! He wouldn't do that."

"That is what all parents say when their adolescent children cannot be found at the resort, but they always turn up by morning."

"You don't understand!" Ezekiel's frustration mounted and his volume increased steadily. "My son doesn't have a rebellious bone in his body. He would not run away! Now, are you going to do something about this or do I have to go out there and look for him myself?"

The officer sighed and fished out a form from his desk drawer. "Here, you can fill out a missing persons report and I will file it with the others."

Elizabeth's questioning eyes held disillusionment. "The others?"

"Yes, the ones that were solved the next day when the missing person showed up again after enjoying the island nightlife."

Ezekiel's formidable gaze narrowed dangerously. He snatched the form from the officer and thrust it at his wife. "Here, fill this out while I start looking for Rylie."

"But," she stammered, "what if... I don't know how... Where will you..."

He took her gently by the arms. "I'll meet you back at the resort in an hour. If we haven't found him by then, I'll phone the Australian authorities."

Elizabeth nodded and leaned on the counter to fill out the form. Ezekiel strode from the building, propelled by a building sense of panic. This was a nightmare, simply a nightmare!

2

New Year's Day, just off the coast of Pearl Island:

The crew filed past the galley serving counter allowing the chef, Able Seaman Joanna Shafer, to load plates with scrambled eggs, bacon and toast. She passed them over one at a time.

The mood was significantly dampened as a result of furlough on Pearl Island for New Year's celebrations. Seaman Nathaniel Underwood and radio operator Jeffrey Williams, Woody and Jaffa to the boys, squinted under the bright florescent lighting as they shuffled forward in line.

Joey suppressed a knowing smile and ensured her serving spoon made a loud clang on Jaffa's plate. Both men cringed.

She recognised the symptoms of a hangover. "What's the matter guys? Did you party a little too hard?"

"You're a cruel woman," Woody grumbled and scuffed his way to a table full of men in equal misery in the junior sailors' mess.

"Wipe that disgustingly happy smile off your face," Jaffa growled, albeit the glint of amusement in his green eyes removed the sting from his comment.

"Yeah, it ought to be illegal to be that cheerful after a big night out," Chief Petty Officer Jason Wilkinson added his remark.

"Well Wilko, some of us can handle our drinks and some of

us can't." Joey shrugged pragmatically.

The chief engineer looked her over and shook his head. She was slim and petite. Her undeniably Asian features, along with her long ebony hair pulled back into its usual ponytail, did tend to make her look very young. Joey followed his train of thought. His expression said he could not understand how such a slip of a woman could drink so much and not feel the effect of it.

Wilko moved on and the executive officer stepped up while she filled his plate. She could not help the sparkle in her brown eyes.

Lieutenant Joshua Donnelly studied her speculatively. "Tell me, Joey, what was it you were drinking last night?"

Joey's face lit with an impish grin. "Apple cider."

The executive officer burst into laughter and took the plate she offered.

She looked regretful. "Like I said, some of us can handle our drinks and some of us can't. I just didn't say what the drink was." She winked conspiratorially which brought forth another laugh from the dark haired, blue-eyed officer. He carried his meal to the wardroom.

Joey caught herself before her admiring gaze could follow his retreating back. She forced her eyes to the sailor next in line. It was Seaman Corrado Pugliese, otherwise known as Coz. At nineteen, he was the youngest member of the crew of twenty-one aboard the HMAS Hartfield, an Australian Armidale Class patrol boat.

Coz's usually warm brown eyes were bloodshot and squinting, evidence that he hadn't slept and was enduring a splitting headache.

"What would your catholic mama say if she could see you

now, Coz? What are you doing getting a hangover?" Joey punctuated her sisterly reprimand with several whacks of her serving spoon to his arm over the counter.

"Hey Joey!" He stepped back from the onslaught. "Take it easy! I just had a couple of drinks with the boys. So did you!"

The cook fixed him with a motherly scowl. "Do I look hung over to you, Cozzi? I don't drink alcohol, and if you're smart, you'll steer clear of it too. Get your little Italian backside in here and help me out."

Coz was well aware she was more bark than bite and started to protest. "But I'm starving!"

"So am I, but we've got a job to do." Joey loaded a plate for the sailor behind him, passing it over the counter.

It was Petty Officer Jay Lonigan, the bosun. His large and imposing stature was tempered by loveable blue eyes that were crinkled at the corners with a huge smile.

"She bossing you around again, Seaman? When are you gonna be a man and stand up to her?"

Joey's gaze narrowed dangerously. "Lon, you leave Coz alone."

"Or what?" He leaned on the counter, his smiling eyes challenging her.

The feisty chef wasn't buying it. She calmly picked up a nearby peppershaker and raised it over his plate. The enormous bosun quickly snatched up his breakfast and scooted out of the way.

Coz snorted and half smiled. "Like you just did?" He headed for the galley entrance.

"Point taken." Lon grinned amiably and went to sit with his colleagues in the wardroom. Joey just shook her head and turned to the next sailor, ready to do battle.

Petty Officer Isaac Farmer held his hands up in surrender and smiled in amusement. "Whoa Joey, I'll use my manners."

Her expression softened instantly. She had a sisterly soft spot for the red-headed coxswain. He was married with three young children; a set of twins in kindergarten and a six-month-old baby.

"You always do." She gave him a double helping and passed him his breakfast.

Farmer beamed at his plate towering with eggs and extra bacon. "That's the reason why boys!"

His comrades behind him in line grumbled good-natured protests, to which Farmer shrugged and gave them a that's-how-it-goes look. Coz entered the galley and donned an apron. In record time the crew was fed, except for the captain and navigator who would eat theirs when Lieutenant Donnelly and Jaffa relieved them on the bridge.

Joey was grateful when the morning rush eased off and she and Coz could sit down to their own meal. She was starved as usual.

~

New Years Day, near the Pearl Islands in the Coral Sea:

Forty-three year old Captain Dave Mickleson exchanged a smile with his second in command, also his long time friend, Phillip Sullivan. Nearby, Dave's sixteen year old daughter Charlotte, Charlie to most, was getting her first lesson at the helm of the massive cargo ship, The Kelly-Ann.

"She's got her mother's looks but her father's love of the sea," Phillip commented.

"Tell me about it!" The fatherly pride in Dave's expression belied his dry tone. "She's been begging to come along on a voyage for years and I've always put her off. This time it's just a short trip down the coast and she had school holidays. I had no excuse. I certainly can't say she's too young any-more."

Phillip chuckled, his eyes also fixed on the tall brunette wearing a t-shirt and jeans and holding the wheel. Beside her was helmsman Warren Jonson, giving her a rundown of the ship's equipment and capabilities.

"When I think of how-" The captain's remark was cut short by the sound of automatic gunfire on the deck outside.

"What in the-" Phillip started to exclaim.

Suddenly the door to the helm crashed open against the wall and two dark skinned men charged in, armed with auto-matic weapons.

Warren reflexively pushed Charlie behind him with a strong arm, his large frame blocking her from view.

"Drop to the floor!" the first intruder shouted. His long black hair was pulled away from his face by a bandana looped around his forehead and tied at the back. His well-muscled, tattooed chest showed beneath a shabby black cotton vest that was unbuttoned. His pants were also black cotton and bare feet protruded from the ends.

His comrade wore a loose sleeveless black shirt without a collar and his trousers were distinctly military. Across the bridge of his nose and running toward his left ear was a long nasty scar. Both sets of dark eyes glimmered menacingly.

When no one moved, the first intruder raised his weap-on to the ceiling and let loose a burst of gunfire. Charlie screamed and covered her ears and the other three men started in fright. Eyes wide, they hastily obeyed, dropping first to their knees and then to their stomachs. The teenager followed their example and did as she was told. Dave knew without a doubt that they were all about to die.

"What do you want?" He injected anger into his tone to cover the terror he was feeling. "This is just a cargo vessel."

"We want what you have on board," the pirate with the bandana replied in clear English and his lips curled into a sadistic smile. His enunciation held only a hint of native accent. "Cover them," he commanded the one with the scar on his face.

Scar-face trained his automatic weapon upon the men while the one calling the shots swung his over his shoulder on a strap. He then took a two-way radio from his waistband.

He pressed the talk button with his thumb and spoke. "Sadewa, do you copy?"

"Yes. We are in the cargo hold like you said, but there are no crates labelled 'rice'. Where do we look now?" another male voice returned amidst static.

"It may be on the main deck inside the shipping containers."

The second in command and the captain exchanged puzzled glances. Whoever these men were, they were after something specific. But why risk a hijacking for a few crates of rice?

"Copy that."

"Now what happens?" Dave asked, fearing the answer yet needing to know.

The pirate in the bandana eyed him with a sinister smile. "We wait."

Minutes of agonising silence ticked by. Gunfire rattled

inside the ship's belly. The handheld radio crackled to life and then an adrenaline charged voice barked, "Abandon ship! Abandon ship!"

The rat-a-tat-tat of gunfire was growing louder and closer.

"Take the girl!" the pirate in charge demanded as he peered warily out the doorway. He watched as two of his men ran for the railing and leapt overboard, followed then by a third.

Dave got to his knees, desperate to keep his daughter out of harm's way. "No, take me instead!"

"We shall take you both." The one with the bandana reached for Dave's collar and dragged him to his feet, even as Scar-face wrenched Charlie by the arm through the doorway onto the deck.

Dave tried to resist. "No!"

A gun muzzle pressed firmly into his back.

"Last chance for you to cooperate." The villain's cold tone sent a shiver down his spine.

He suppressed the urge to fight and allowed himself to be shoved from the helm to the upper railing. He had to stay with his daughter, no matter the cost.

Charlie was thrust overboard and then followed by Scar-face. It was a clear summer's day, and for miles in all directions, Dave could see only calm blue sea. As he looked down, he noticed a zodiac nudging the ship's hull, into which the pirates were now scrambling.

While he was assessing the scene, a violent push sent him toppling over the rail. He plummeted into the ocean below and kicked to the surface. Where was Charlie? There was a second splash behind him and he guessed that the pirate with the bandana had leapt overboard after him. The zodiac powered toward them and two sets of tattooed arms reached down and pulled Dave roughly into the boat.

Coughing and spluttering on the floor of the vessel, he managed a sweeping glance of all on board the small craft. Five pirates altogether; one at the wheel, two hauling their leader in, another pinning Dave to the floor and the fifth holding Charlie, using her as a human shield at the rear of the boat.

The moment their boss was aboard, the zodiac turned and fled. Dave had a pretty good idea why, seeing the way the brigand at the rear of the boat was hiding behind his daughter. Behind them, the crew of The Kelly-Ann was standing at the rail, and one rough looking sailor was aiming an automatic weapon at the zodiac. It had to have been confiscated from the intruders.

As the smaller vessel sped away, the leader righted himself and sat on the rim of the boat, holding onto small hand grips that were positioned at intervals along the edge.

"Tie them up."

Dave met his daughter's terrified gaze as their hands were roughly bound with thin rope. "It'll be alright." He was not at all convinced that he was telling the truth. "Where are we going?"

He was completely ignored.

"Did you find it?" The driver glanced over his sun-bronzed shoulder at his comrades.

Dave studied his captors. They were all dressed in rather shabby clothing, well worn and dark in colour, and all appeared to be native to the Pearl Islands. Scar-face sat beside him on his right. The brutal fellow in charge was on his left, all sitting on the rim of the boat. The driver had his hair cropped closely to his scalp, and upon his upper arm was a tattoo of a venomous snake. Upon the back of his hand was a picture of a huge ugly spider. Both were deadly Dave supposed, just like the man that wore them.

Another pirate sat on the rim at the back of the boat, also hanging onto hand holds. He was small of stature, yet stocky. His eyes were so dark they were almost black, almost as black as the soul staring out of them. The third was the villain that had used Charlie as a human shield. He differed from the rest in that his eyes were as blue as the shallow depths of the waters they were now entering. He was sitting beside the teenager on the right rim of the zodiac. He was the one that answered.

"One of them got my gun and started shooting. The others came at us in a mob and we had no choice but to get out of there."

His angry eyes betrayed a glint of fear. Clearly errors were not tolerated.

"You are lucky I took these two hostage or I would be killing you right now," the pirate with the bandana remarked with a chilling lack of emotion. "We will seek a ransom."

Each man smiled except the one who had cost them the merchandise. He looked at Dave and breathed a sigh of relief.

"Look Dad, an island," Charlie spoke for the first time since the abduction. Her wide blue eyes, so light in colour they were almost lilac, watched a green mass of mountains and jungle rise from the depths of the Coral Sea. Dave wondered if it was inhabited, and hoped with every fibre of his quaking being that someone there might be able to help them.

3

"Hey, I saw that look you gave the XO before he walked off with his breakfast," Coz remarked with a cheeky grin later that morning as he dried and put away the last dish.

The galley had cleared of all personnel so that now only he and Joey remained.

"And what look would that be?" she asked mildly as she mixed a huge bowl of cookie dough.

"That you're-the-best-thing-since-sliced-bread look." The cheeky teenager grinned. His short hair was thick and black and his skin was as tanned as Joey's. However, there the similarities ended. Where she was slender, he was well muscled and a whole head taller.

She gave the wooden spoon a heavy clunk on the rim of the bowl and turned to face her friend with her other hand on her hip. He was more like a beloved brother than a workmate, making the hours in the galley a whole lot of fun.

"You were so hung over you wouldn't know what you saw."

Coz smiled knowingly. He pointed to her feigned scowl and chuckled. "I can read you like a book."

Joey suppressed a smile. He was incorrigible. "Is that so?"

"Yep. When you kick harder, it means I'm getting closer to the truth."

Joey snorted in a most unladylike fashion. This only made Coz grin triumphantly.

"Joey-love, you're enamoured with the XO." He sidled to the steel bench where she was working.

"Call me Joey-love again and I'll get you in a headlock."

"Joey loves the lieutenant." He used a sing-song voice like a primary school kid.

The cook's eyes narrowed, a good indicator he should back off. "You be careful what you say, whippersnapper. Spreading scuttlebutt is a serious offence."

Coz's smile was cocky. "I'm not spreading a thing. I've come straight to the source and I can tell she's undergoing some serious denial." He reached a finger into the bowl as he spoke.

Joey swatted his hand away. "You want some of this?" A telltale mischievous gleam entered her velvety brown eyes, eyes most guys fell all over themselves for. But not Coz. She knew she was like a sister to him, very similar to the two he had left behind in Cairns when he set sail on the HMAS Hartfield. Barring her Asian looks of course.

He shrugged. "Sure."

"After teasing me about the lieutenant, you want some cookie dough?" She placed her hand on her hip again, the other surreptitiously scooping a handful from the bowl.

A suspicious light entered his eyes and he took a step backward. Joey moved like lightning, jumping and hooking her left elbow around the back of his neck. She used her weight to draw his head down to knee level. Before he had time to react, he was in a firm headlock and she was stuffing cookie dough into his wide-open protesting trap.

"How's it taste, Cozzi? Is that enough to whet your appetite for morning tea?" She squashed the last glob in her hand into his mouth.

He half laughed and half chewed to keep from choking.

"Is everything alright in here?" a deep male voice asked dubiously from the doorway.

Joey recognised it immediately and snapped to attention, as did Coz. Commander Shane Kelly stepped into the galley and surveyed his galley crew with what appeared to be barely restrained amusement.

"Yes sir." Joey stared straight ahead and tried desperately to rein in a smile. "Coz was just taste testing the cookie dough."

"So I see." The captain's green eyes were creased at the corners. Taking into consideration the two smile lines along his cheeks, they gave evidence of a long time sense of humour.

His age was difficult to pinpoint. He could be anywhere between forty and sixty. His ginger hair was littered with grey and beginning to recede. He was not overly tall or handsome, and yet there was something about him that won Joey's loyalty. Perhaps it was his commanding presence, or maybe his kindness and wit. She wasn't sure. All she knew was that she liked him. He reminded her of her father.

"I have to say, sir, that it's quite good. Although a few extra chocolate chips wouldn't go astray," Coz commented, also standing at attention.

"Is that right?" Shane Kelly seemed to struggle hiding a smile of his own. "As you were."

Joey relaxed and went back to mixing. Coz wiped dough from around his mouth with a sleeve. "Can I get you something, sir?"

"Thanks Seaman Pugliese, but I just came for coffee." The commander opened the cupboard above the stove and took down a mug. He was reaching for the coffee tin when an announcement came over the ship's intercom.

"Commander Kelly to the bridge." It sounded like Lieutenant Donnelly.

The commander sighed and replaced the mug. "So much for a brew." He sighed and strode from the galley.

Joey and Coz exchanged glances and released the laughter they had been holding. She clouted her best mate across the back of his head.

"Needs more chocolate chips hey?"

Coz only laughed.

"Take over with these cookies will you?" She crossed to the cupboard with the mugs and turned to point a warning finger at him. "And no more taste testing!"

"Don't worry, you gave me my fill." He took up the mixing spoon in his right and the bowl in his left.

Joey chuckled and made the commander a coffee just the way he liked it. She was headed for the galley door when the ship's two diesel engines roared and the vessel tilted slightly with the sudden increase in power.

They exchanged surprised glances.

"Feels like we're going at top speed."

"I guess something's come up. I'll go find out."

Joey carefully carried the commander's coffee through the maze of passages and stairways until she reached the final one. Even from the base of the stairs to the bridge, she could hear disquiet in the voices above and feel their tension. Something was most definitely afoot.

She balanced the mug, allowing for the rocking motion of the vessel, and made it up the stairs without spilling a drop. Standing just inside the bridge, she scanned the room fitted with state of the art computer systems, radar, communications and low light optical equipment.

Sitting at the radar and navigation station was Lieutenant Ben Shepparton, a man of about twenty-eight. Jaffa was in his chair at the radio desk. The executive officer was studying a chart spread beneath glass, atop a flat bench next to the waist high wall which separated the bridge from the stairway. Commander Kelly was reading a print out of information probably sent by command back in Cairns.

Joey waited silently out of the way, sensing their unease. The commander turned to the radio operator, his expression dark with concern.

"Put an announcement over for the crew to assemble on the quarter deck, Jaffa. Shep, how long until we rendezvous with The Kelly-Ann?"

Shep glanced at his equipment, made a few mental calculations and then answered. "At our top speed of twenty-five knots, we should arrive in two and a half hours, sir."

"Alright. Keep us on this heading while I brief the men. The XO has the con." Commander Kelly started for the stairs. It was then he noticed Joey.

She grimaced sheepishly and held out his coffee, knowing now was not really the time. The commander smiled warmly and received the mug.

"Thanks Joey." He took a long sip and sighed with satisfaction. "I needed that. Things are about to get hairy."

"What's going on, sir?"

"Follow me and you'll find out." He preceded her down the stairs. As she followed, an announcement went over the ship's intercom for the crew to assemble.

The island loomed ahead, wild with lush green jungle. Now sitting on the edge of the speeding zodiac, Charlie could clearly see it was larger than she had first thought. Because of its size, it appeared closer than it actually was. She guessed it to be roughly a kilometre away. Her initial terror abated enough for her usual curiosity to peak.

"What's the island called?"

"It's better they know as little as possible," Scar-face commented and the leader nodded from his place on the zodiac edge.

"What is that?" The driver squinted at an obstacle up ahead and his eyes suddenly widened in fear. "A rock!" He veered to port.

The three men along the left side toppled into the boat and the man at the rear held onto a handhold and managed to stay aboard. Dave fell hard against the rubber hulled floor. Unable to grip anything on the right rim with her hands bound, Charlie flipped backward. With a surprised screech, she hit the water hard and disappeared beneath the surface.

4

The pirate beside Charlie fell also, only his right hand kept a firm grasp of a handhold along the rim. He toppled into the water but managed to haul himself back into the zodiac, dripping wet and sending the driver a murderous look. The man only grinned in return and kept driving, now thoroughly enjoying the humorous incident.

"Charlotte! Where's Charlotte?" Dave struggled to his knees and scanned the foamy surface behind the boat.

Nothing. She had vanished.

"She's gone overboard. Will you stop the boat?" Scar-face appeared somewhat disgruntled.

"We cannot," the leader replied pragmatically. "We might be followed. We need as much space as possible between the ship and us." He indicated for the driver to speed up with a dispassionate flick of his wrist. "We still have one hostage to ransom."

"But her hands are tied! She'll drown!" Dave walked on his knees to the back of the boat and frantically searched the rippling surface for any sign of his daughter.

"It was a crate, moron, not a rock," Sadewa informed the driver dryly and dropped onto his backside on the zodiac floor.

"You can't just leave her!" Dave screamed angrily and rose, intending to dive overboard and go after her.

A mad scramble ensued and a tangle of arms and legs

24

grabbed him. He kicked and gouged until finally a solid fist crashed down on the crown of his head. The nightmare around him evaporated into darkness and he slumped to the floor.

~

Charlie gripped a rock on the ocean bed with stiff fingers to keep from surfacing. The vivid colours of the coral around her was completely lost on her oxygen starved brain. She could see the zodiac churning water into the distance and then her clouded vision lost sight of it altogether. She held her breath for as long as she could, feeling her lungs burning and quelling their impulse to suck in air that simply was not there.

Finally spots began to dance before her eyes and she kicked to the surface, using her bound hands to claw handfuls of water and propel her upward. Thankfully the water was only four or five metres deep. Her head broke the surface and she gasped. With several more breaths the dizzy sensation left and she was able to look around.

The zodiac sped into the distance, and from what she could see, the men appeared to be in a struggle with each other. Several metres to her right, water lapped lazily against a medium sized wooden crate. She took a deep breath and ducked under again.

If she could see them then they would be able to see her. The minute they stopped fighting, or doing whatever it was they were doing, they might glance back again and she would be caught. She would be of more use to her father if she could get help and make known his location.

She swam toward the crate, able to see its underside bobbing in the water. She surfaced and gasped for breath, feeling herself tiring. If she didn't free her hands soon she would become exhausted and drown. She hung onto the crate, positioning it between her and the zodiac. What now? What could she use to cut the rope binding her hands?

A slow smile parted her lips. She took a deep breath and allowed herself to sink while she awkwardly fished in her pocket for the multi tool Phillip had given her when they began the voyage.

"Every sailor needs a knife. This is even better." He had passed her the metal instrument tucked into a black pouch.

Her shaking fingers felt the leather pouch and pulled it free of her pocket. No easy feat with hands bound and no incoming oxygen. But she couldn't stay afloat while fishing it out, and her wet jeans made the task all the more challenging.

Finally with the tool in her grasp, she surfaced and latched onto the crate. Her hands wanted to fumble and she knew she would drop it if they did. She drew a calming breath and with slow, deliberate movements, removed the tool from its pouch, selected the knife blade and flicked it open.

She peered around the crate for a view of the zodiac. It had gone around a point. They had left her for dead. She smiled to herself. Good. They hadn't counted on a canny teenager's ability to survive, and she was determined to do just that.

Charlie held the knife upside down in her right hand and with slow, small movements painstakingly sliced through the rope. After about five minutes, it gave way and she was able to unwind it and slip her hands out.

She pocketed the multi tool and discarded the rope. Somehow she had to rescue her father, and that meant from now on she needed to be thinking as deviously as his captors.

She glanced toward the island looming tall and beautiful a kilometre or so away. She leaned her torso on the crate, got a firm grip and began kicking her legs, steering directly toward its white sandy beach.

5

"What about the airport? Someone might try to escape with him by plane," Ezekiel suggested, again standing anxiously at the police station counter.

"That is not likely," the officer at the front desk replied logically.

He was a different policeman than the one the Hunters had encountered the night before. He was younger, perhaps in his late twenties. He was also of native islander descent, if his mellow brown skin and dark hair and eyes were any indication. He spoke clear English, as did the majority of people in the Pearl Islands.

"I was reading over the report you filled out only half an hour ago and cannot fathom why a search was not carried out on the spot. I have already alerted airport security to this situation, although I doubt anyone would dare take your son to a public place where he might cause a scene," the young man explained, rising from his seat behind the front desk. "It is more likely they would try to abscond with him by boat."

"What about charter planes?" Elizabeth leaned on the desk, desperation in her anxious eyes.

"No, it is unlikely." He began making a cup of tea at the kettle on a table against the far left wall. "He would be too easy to track. Whoever took the boy will either hide away on the island, or slip out of the harbour quietly by boat." He glanced over his shoulder as he dipped a teabag in a mug of hot water. "We will search the island. I have already dis-patched two men to investigate while I have been making phone calls here."

Ezekiel absently noticed the casual way with which the officer made the beverage and wondered if he really would be as helpful as he claimed. His calm actions indicated other-wise.

The young man poured milk into the mug, removed the teabag and carried the drink around the front desk. "Here." He offered it to Elizabeth.

Ezekiel saw kindness soften his business-like gaze and watched his wife gratefully accept the cup.

"Thank you."

Ezekiel felt momentarily guilty for his uncharitable assess-ment of the man.

"Can I offer you a drink, Mr. Hunter?"

Ezekiel shook his head. He could do with a hot coffee, but he refused to dally seeing to his own comfort when his son was out there somewhere in the clutches of a criminal. "Is there some way of tracking vessels that leave the bay?"

The officer smiled cannily. "Yes and no. We shall ask around the docks. That is where I was headed in the next twenty minutes. However, I think our best bet would be to contact HMAS Hartfield that pulled out of port early this morning. They will be able to take a look around at sea."

Ezekiel's brows shot upward in surprise and hope bur-geoned within him. "Make the call."

~

"Men, it seems this isn't going to be a normal patrol,"

Commander Kelly addressed the crew assembled on the quarter deck in three rows. "This morning we received a mayday from The Kelly-Ann, a large Australian cargo vessel sailing just off the Pearl Islands. She was hijacked by pirates who were searching her for something specific. The crew are not sure what it was.

"They overpowered them but the pirates escaped with the captain and his teenage daughter. When we broke off contact, the crew were making preparations to begin negotiations to get the hostages back. I've briefed the Admiral back at base and he has given us the go ahead to rendezvous with The Kelly-Ann and look into this." The captain's calm gaze rested on each of his crew one at a time.

"Sir, do we have orders to recover the hostages?" the bosun asked, seeming ready and willing for action.

"Not as yet. If negotiations prove successful, it may save a very bloody battle. At the moment our orders are to search the vessel for whatever it is the pirates were after. However, those orders could change within the hour." Commander Kelly clasped his hands behind his back.

"But sir, the longer we wait, the more time they have to put distance between us," Wilko observed.

"Admiral Broderick believes that they will probably demand a ransom. That's why they took Captain Mickleson and his daughter Charlotte instead of just fleeing."

Joey noted that understanding cleared many of the confused frowns on the crews' faces around her, while Wilko looked put out that there would not be a chase.

"I'm sending a boarding party of nine onto The Kelly-Ann. Lieutenant Donnelly will lead it. I want everyone armed in case we bump into these pirates, although they would be mad to take on a navy warship.

"As soon as you are dismissed, put on a side arm. Would these crew members please remain behind to prepare for boarding." Commander Kelly glanced at each sailor as he said their name. "Lon, Farmer, Woody, Ollie, Coz, Corey, Daz, Katie and Wes."

Joey listened to her roommate's name being called and knew she would be pleased. Able Seaman Katherine Dean was a sailor through and through. She loved the navy and lived for action. Then Joey thought of Coz. He would be over the moon. She sneaked a peek at his face and smiled. Pride shone from his sparkling brown eyes and his chest had puffed out another inch.

"Dismissed."

The crew headed to fetch side arms.

"Hey Switch!" Wilko grinned and elbowed Leading Seaman Sarah young, the electronics technician.

She was nicknamed for her penchant for tinkering with anything that was electrical.

"D'you reckon it's a good idea for Joey to be packin' lead?"

Sarah grinned sideways at the cheeky cook. "It could be a bit dangerous."

Joey wore an easy going smile and gave her a playful shove. "What are you talking about? I might get a little more respect in the galley."

"Yeah well, it won't be Cozzi's." Switch glanced over her shoulder at the nineteen year old listening intently to the captain's detailed instructions.

Joey turned and studied him, exchanging a grin with the other woman. "Yeah, he's proud as punch."

"I reckon his buttons will burst any minute now."

It was Coz's first boarding.

Wilko smiled broadly and allowed the women to precede him inside. "If he catches sight of those pirates, he'll wish he was back in the galley."

6

Rylie's stomach rolled ominously. It felt like he was rocking. The haze shrouding his brain was starting to clear and he was becoming more aware of his surroundings. He focused on his legs and was able to bend them at the knees. What was wrong with him? Why couldn't he function properly?

He rolled onto his right side and struggled up onto an elbow. The offending limb would not support his weight and he collapsed back against the mattress.

Mattress... This did not feel like his bed! Where was he? He forced his glassy eyes wide open and blinked to focus. The ceiling was made of wooden planks held up by support beams. A porthole in the wall to his right let in shafts of light. The floor was wooden and dusted with a thin smattering of fish scales here and there. The room was rank and smelled like it hadn't breathed fresh air in decades.

His dull senses finally picked up the low grumble of an engine chugging lazily along, and was that water lapping against the wall? Or was it a hull?

He sucked in a deep breath in an attempt to clear his addled mind and tried to push up onto his elbow again. Directly in front of him was a ladder that led to a hatch in the ceiling. He had to get up. He had to somehow get out of this place.

From leaning on his elbow, he was able to sit up. He swayed with the gentle motion of the prow of a boat slicing through ocean swells. He stared longingly at the hatch. It seemed so far away, yet he had to reach it. He just had to!

Suddenly the hatch was thrown back and a dark shadow climbed down the ladder.

"Who are you?" Rylie forced the slurred words past dry, parched lips. "Where am I?"

The hulking figure crossed the small room and with one huge paw pushed Rylie back onto the mattress. The boy was as weak as a kitten and could not struggle.

"So it's wearing off is it?"

Rylie focused on the face bent over him. It was partially hidden by a dark chest length beard. A bulbous nose peeked over long whiskers, and peering from above it were two brown eyes, almost amber when they caught a shaft of light from the window. The leathery face eased into a sadistic smile. Just below his right eye on his cheekbone was a small tattoo of a skull.

"Sleep tight, son." A deep voice chuckled.

Rylie frowned in puzzlement and tried to sit up again. The large hand pushed heavily against his shoulder and the kidnapper drew a needle from his pocket. He removed his hand long enough to uncap the tip and push airlocks from the chemical inside the syringe.

"No!" Rylie raised his hands to stop its descent toward his arm.

With a cruel chuckle, the kidnapper leaned his torso against his right shoulder, effectively pinning Rylie down.

"I don't want that stuff in me! Don't!" He banged against the man's broad back. "Let me go! I want to go home!"

"Sorry sonny, not yet. Maybe not ever." He grabbed Rylie's right arm, which was stretched before him, and inserted the needle.

"No!" the sixteen year old screamed, even as he felt that strange sensation steal over him again.

Within minutes, his limbs lost power and he was paralysed and absolutely helpless. Was he going to die? He hated being at the mercy of this heartless man! Who was he and why was he doing this?

"Just relax and pretty soon it will all be over." The villain's easygoing tone did nothing to comfort him.

"Let me go." Rylie's words came out slurred. He was quickly losing the ability to speak. In a few minutes, every muscle in his body would be completely useless.

In answer to his plea, footsteps retreated and the hatch dropped shut. A bolt slid into place.

Please God, get me out of here?

~

Coz jemmied the lid off a waist high wooden crate and frowned. How was he supposed to search this? The rice was in sealed sacks. The heavy steel shipping container door creaked behind him and he spun around.

"Don't you close that door on us, Lon, or so help me..." He let the threat hang in the air.

Petty Officer Lonigan only grinned and made the door creak forebodingly. The boatswain's mate, Able Seaman Oliver Startori, turned from the crate beside him and glared at the bosun.

"Coz may be too nice to follow through on a threat, but I'm not. I don't care that you're a higher ranking sailor than me, Lon. If you close that door, I'll thrash you to within an inch of your life when I get out."

It seemed unlikely with the enormous size of the bosun compared to Ollie's smaller build. Nevertheless, Ollie was still tall and very strong.

Lon smiled mischievously, always a big tease. "I'd like to see you try."

The claustrophobic sailors searching the shipping container exchanged annoyed glances. They were on the edge enough with pirates in the area without having to worry about their rascally comrade.

"Come on, Ollie, let's just get this done." Coz hauled the top sack of rice upright. He took his pocket knife from the zip pocket on his left pant leg, opened it and sliced into the sack. Rice spilled onto the floor. Ignoring the mess, he plunged his hand deeper into the sack and felt around. Just when he was about to withdraw it, his fingers landed upon something smooth and impenetrable.

"Hey Ollie, I think I've found something."

The twenty-five year old glanced over at him. "What is it?"

"Plastic." Coz dug deeper and got a firm grip on what felt like a package. It was pliable, almost like a bag of flour. He pulled it out and shook it free of rice.

Lon wandered curiously to his side and stared at the plastic bag containing white powder.

"What is it?" Coz asked innocently.

Lon's eyes narrowed knowingly and he snatched it from the younger man. He studied it in the light spilling into the shipping container.

"It's drugs."

Coz's brows shot upward in surprise. Ollie held out his hand, silently requesting the pocket knife. Coz passed it over and watched as Ollie slashed open a sack from his crate. He plunged his hand into the rice while Coz and Lon waited.

"There's more in here too. Coz, dig deeper."

"I'll inform the XO." Lon's usually gleaming eyes were dark with the troubling discovery.

~

"Yes sir, they were after drugs. Lieutenant Donnelly thinks it's opium," Commander Kelly spoke into the satellite phone on the bridge.

Lieutenant Shepparton and radio operator Jaffa Williams both raised surprised brows and exchanged glances, as they listened to half of the conversation between the captain and Admiral Broderick back in Cairns.

"Yes sir, I believe that would be the wisest course of action. In the meantime, what do we do about the hostages? ... No sir, no ransom has been demanded yet. ... Yes sir, I believe we can handle that. ... Yes sir. I'll be in touch." Commander Kelly replaced the phone in its cradle.

"So, what are our orders, sir?" Shep asked the man standing with his back to them, staring out at The Kelly-Ann just off their starboard side.

The captain clasped his hands behind his back and turned to them. His smile was pure devilment. "We have orders to confiscate the drugs, hand them over to the federal police who will be taking charge here, and then go catch us some pirates."

Jaffa grinned and leaned back in his swivel chair. "And I thought they'd give us something difficult to do."

7

Charlie dropped onto the sand and stared at aqua waves curling onto the shore. What should she do now? She had spent hours walking along the beach hoping she might find a small fishing port around each bend. But she hadn't. From all appearances, the island was uninhabited.

Well, all except for some pirates, she mused. Surely they have a hideout here somewhere.

She picked up a small shell and tossed it toward the waves. Crystal clear water rushed up the sand, licked up the shell, and quickly withdrew. It would be getting dark soon and she needed a place to shelter and hide for the night. She fished in her other pocket, felt the small round object there and smiled. She pulled it out and was relieved to find that it was not waterlogged. It was the compass her father had given her when she turned ten.

"What else have you got in those pockets of yours?" she heard her mother's voice echo from the recent past. She had been fossicking through her jeans before tossing them in the washing machine.

"Just enough to keep me out of trouble."

Sandra Mickleson's delighted laugh bounced off the walls of Charlie's mind and her throat clogged with tears. She had been filled with excitement at the beginning of this voyage, and now it had fallen drastically apart. Was her father alright? Would she ever see her family again?

"Stop it! You have a mission and there is no time to sit

around feeling sorry for yourself!"

With that settled, she jumped to her feet and studied her compass. "Okay, if that direction is north and I'm headed into the jungle there, my heading is sixteen degrees northeast."

She looked up at the tropical trees towering over her. Their large green leaves rustled in the gentle breeze. The ocean lapped in a lazy cycle against the shore behind her. Suddenly the jungle seemed forbidding and eerily quiet.

Charlie mentally shook herself. "You've seen way too many movies." She strode forward into the wilderness.

~

"What's going on?"

The caller's demanding tone sent a shiver up the executive's spine.

"It's on the news! The Kelly-Ann has been hijacked by pirates!"

The tall, debonair businessman sank into his leather desk chair in his luxurious city office and sighed. "Yes. The second in command has been keeping me updated."

"What's this about the HMAS Hartfield finding drugs on board? And how did pirates find out about the shipment anyway?"

The executive cradled his head in his free hand and wished the pounding behind his eyes would stop. "I don't know."

"How many more kids have to disappear to get the message through to you? Botch this up and the boy dies."

The line disconnected and the executive stared at the telephone as though it were poison. He asked himself why he continued to go along with the plan. Then he remembered the money. For once he questioned whether it was really worth it. He resigned himself to the fact he had no choice.

~

"You look like you're feeling proud of yourself." Joey watched Coz don an apron and step to the counter to help her serve dinner that evening.

His eyes shone with pride. "And why not? I helped find one of the biggest stashes of opium being smuggled into Australia in a decade."

"You weren't the only one that discovered it, Coz," Lon pointed out from the other side of the counter.

"I said I helped. I didn't say I found it all."

He dumped a serving spoon full of mashed potatoes onto the bosun's plate. He passed it to Joey who added a scoop of greens and a thick slice of roast beef.

"Come on, Lon, give credit where it's due," she replied reasonably.

Lon grunted, yet his blue eyes glittered with humour.

"Wow Joey," Farmer commented as she and Coz loaded his plate next. "You've outdone yourself again."

Joey smiled with pleasure and added an extra slice of beef. "That's what I like to hear."

"I saw that!" Shep objected as Coz heaped potato onto the navigator's plate. "Do I get another piece?"

Joey raised a single perfectly shaped brow, her eyes somewhat cool. "Not when your first words to me all day are a complaint." She feigned a miffed expression and gave him only one slice.

"Oh come on Joey darlin'." He slipped into an Irish brogue

and winked. "Yi know I love yi."

She chuckled and relented. "Only because I feed you."

"That's a bit harsh."

She passed him his plate, totally unimpressed by his wounded expression.

Lieutenant Joshua Donnelly stepped up next to collect his meal with a friendly smile in place. "This smells good. You did well today, Coz."

The young man in question loaded his plate.

"Yes, excellent work." Commander Kelly surprised him with the comment as he took his place in line. His brows were drawn together, suggesting that he had something troubling on his mind.

"Any news on the status of The Kelly-Ann?" the XO asked conversationally.

Joey and Coz listened intently as they continued to dish up food.

"The Australian Federal Police have finally arrived. The Kelly-Ann will remain at anchor just off the coast of Pearl Island while they investigate and resolve the matter." Commander Kelly took his full plate from the counter.

"And the pirates?"

"We've got orders to locate them."

"Locate them? Does that mean we have permission to capture them and recover the hostages?" The XO moved away from the counter to allow the men through.

"Not as yet. If we go in with guns blazing and they demand a ransom, it could cost the hostages their lives. We're to play this thing one step at a time."

"So what's our first step?"

"The Kelly-Ann was hijacked close to the coasts of both Lila and Gabriel Island, as you know."

The crew around the captain tuned into the conversation curiously.

"We'll dock at Lila Island in a small fishing harbour in the morning and do some investigation of our own. If nothing turns up there, we'll sail to Gabriel. It's almost two times the size of Lila and it's uninhabited, so it might be a little more difficult to search. Either way, I think it's reasonable to assume that the pirates took the hostages to either of those two islands.

"If they're moving around, it will make the search even harder. But with our radar equipment, we should be able to pick up any traffic in the area."

"I'll brief the men after dinner."

"Thanks Lieutenant. I'd better head back up to the bridge. You know what they say. No rest for the wicked."

Lieutenant Donnelly grinned. "Yes sir."

The captain exited the way he had come. Jaffa nudged the XO and waggled his eyebrows. "I don't suppose we'll get a few hours liberty on Lila, sir?"

The executive officer smiled in amusement. "You're a wishful thinker, Jaffa. Besides, who wants liberty when we're fed like kings by our lovely chef and her trusty accomplice?" He directed the last part of his remark to Joey with eyes gleaming in merriment.

"Don't fall for it, Joey!" Shep called across the small space. "He's after extra roast beef."

A few snickers and guffaws accompanied the fun loving banter.

Joey continued serving the men. "Well, he's going the right way about it."

The man in question chuckled and flashed the cook a warm smile. "Why thank you, Joey."

~

Charlie crawled from beneath the large palm tree where she had spread fronds to make a bed the night before, and stood overlooking the landscape before her. It was a rolling mass of mountains to her right and to her left. Straight ahead, the jungle dropped away in a steady descent. At the base of the mountain she stood upon, the ocean lapped at golden sand. Its aqua depths stretched as far as the eye could see in all directions, mirroring the azure dome arching over it. It reminded her of a child's snow globe, only the scene inside was beautifully tropical.

She surveyed the mountainous terrain around her and her wandering gaze halted on a white line of foam churned in the wake of what looked like a fishing vessel. It was a small speck upon the ocean from this height and distance.

She watched it sail away from the coastline on her right, heading southwest. Perhaps other fishermen were in that area too? She had not been able to walk that far yet. Charlie estimated that it would take her perhaps half a day to get there. On the other hand, it could be the pirates' base. If that was the case, she would find her father and help him escape. It certainly wouldn't be easy, but she had every confidence in her ability to do just that.

Charlie had the advantage because they thought she was dead. Using her compass, she set her course for the cove out of which the vessel had sailed, determined to accomplish her self-assigned mission.

~

The entrepreneur lazed in his deck chair on the spacious balcony of his sprawling two-story mansion on Blue Jay Island. He frowned in puzzlement.

His home was perched upon a steady incline, surrounded by tropical jungle, yet high enough to gain an excellent view of the stunning vista stretching to the horizon. The Coral Sea rippled like a sapphire blanket ruffled ever so gently by the wind.

However, the immense beauty before him brought no joy, not with the news of pirates hijacking The Kelly-Ann. If his contact had not alerted anyone to the presence of the smuggled drugs on board, then who had? Had it been a strange coincidence? Not likely, not with television reports detailing the targeted way they had searched the vessel. No, the thieves had known opium was on board and also the label under which it was travelling. But how?

His mind suddenly flashed back a week ago to a dark night in a seedy tavern on Lila Island, not far from Blue Jay in the Pearl Island grouping. He had met with Zacutti to discuss the details of their plan. With understanding came a surge of self-directed anger. How could he have been so foolish? He should have chosen a more secluded place to rendezvous with his right hand man.

The tavern had been rather busy with fishermen and local rabble-rousers, but it only took one pair of ears to pick up the mention of a lucrative drug stash. He should have known better! They had been discreet, but obviously not discreet enough.

A vague recollection of a native islander with a scar running across his cheek sprang to mind. The rough looking character had wandered drunkenly past their secluded table in a shadowed corner on his way to the men's room. Perhaps he had not been drunk at all?

This simple mistake could cost him his whole operation. He consoled himself with the knowledge that his involvement was untraceable. The only person that knew him by name was Zacutti, and he was too good at his job to ever be caught. No, no matter what the navy or the feds found, he was untouchable. The frown between his brows eased as a satisfied smirk tugged at the corners of his mouth.

8

Jaffa handed the satellite phone to the executive officer. The radio operator listened to half of the conversation with a great deal of interest. This was an unusually eventful patrol.

"And you're positive the boy was kidnapped? ... The Southern Star Restaurant? That's rather a public place for an abduction. Was the kidnapper recorded on security tape? ... I see. What are the island police doing to recover him? ... Yes, that certainly would be the way to do it. What kind of vessel are we looking for? ... That doesn't give us much to go on. I'll alert the captain and command in Cairns and we'll get back to you promptly. ... Yes, thank you."

Lieutenant Donnelly handed the receiver to Jaffa and started for the stairs. "The navigator has the con."

He left the men on duty in the bridge to ponder the curious conversation. Shep and Jaffa exchanged glances and shrugged.

~

"I was informed only five minutes ago that the pirates have demanded a ransom for their hostages. Command in Cairns still want us to locate them while Hunter Shipping Lines continues negotiations. Our orders to proceed one step at a time still stand," Commander Kelly explained to the crew assembled on the quarter deck.

The ship sailed between two large cliffs into Abbotsford Cove on Lila Island.

"Another matter of importance has come up that I think you should all be aware of while you're searching Lila. We received a call from the Pearl Island police an hour ago, who informed us about the abduction of a sixteen year old boy named Rylie Hunter. He's the son of Ezekiel Hunter, who iron-ically is the owner of Hunter Shipping Lines. The Kelly-Ann is one of his company's vessels. The boy disappeared new year's eve from the Southern Star Resort on Pearl Island."

Joey's face drained of colour and her heart froze in her chest. Abducted. Unbidden, suppressed memories flooded her consciousness and spots began to dance before her eyes. She sucked in a deep breath and grasped the closest solid object, which happened to be the railing a few inches behind her.

Please Lord, not here? She could feel shock stealing over her, just as it had the other times her past reared its ugly head. *Help me hold it together?* Still the memories came, as fresh as the day it all happened.

A drop of liquid poised on the tip of the needle reflected a reddish glint from the bedside lamp. She watched help-lessly as the syringe lowered menacingly to her right elbow. She groaned in protest and tried to move a hand, an arm... anything to defend herself. It was useless. The drug that was already in her system rendered her paralysed.

She felt the syringe bite into the tender flesh of her inner elbow, then the cold infusion of a foreign chemical entering her blood stream. A strange mixture of euphoria and fear spun her mind out of control and reality slipped away again. Footsteps retreated from the room.

Suddenly voices began screaming and the sound of gunshots penetrated the haze surrounding her brain.

"Did you hit him?"

"I think I winged him just as he ran out the back door."

Footsteps drew near. She wanted to fight, to flee, to call for help. But all she could do was lie there, helpless and vulnerable.

"Sir, I've found her! She's in the bedroom!"

"Is it Jessica Hyndman?" Another voice came close.

"Yes."

"Call an ambulance and let her family know she's safe, and send the rest of the men after the kidnapper."

"Yes sir."

The hostage felt pressure on her wrist and then a gentle hand brushed long ebony hair from her face. "Jessica, can you hear me?"

Yes, I can! her mind screamed, but she could not respond. She was vaguely aware of her limbs but unable to move them.

"If you can hear me, I want you to know you're safe now. I'm senior detective Ben Spencer with the New South Wales Police. Hang in there and we'll get you back to your family."

A single tear slipped from the corner of her closed eyelids.

Able Seaman Katie Dean glanced at Joey curiously. "Are you okay?"

The captain's voice continued in the background. With a valiant effort, Joey managed to control her breathing so that the faint feeling left her. She shoved the disturbing images aside with all of her willpower and offered her roommate a forced smile. Katie did not look convinced, yet she returned her attention to the captain.

"The police are monitoring the airports, but they are unable to track all of the traffic that leaves port. Command in Cairns feels it's more important that we locate the pirates than go looking for a boat that may or may not exist.

"However, if you see or hear anything that might help in recovering the boy, then let me know immediately." Commander Kelly nodded crisply in his usual manner. "Now, you have your orders. Travel in groups of three or four. I'll leave the groupings to Petty Officer Lonigan and Lieutenant Donnelly. Report to them as soon as we've docked.

"A skeleton crew will remain on board. This will include Lieutenant Shepparton, Leading Seaman Williams, Leading Seaman Debartista, Seaman Blackwell, Able Seaman Yusef, Seaman Oldham and myself. Crew dismissed."

Officers and junior sailors alike scattered in different directions. Joey's mind reeled. Of all the days for her to be ordered ashore on a mission, why did it have to be today and why on a case like this? Two kidnappings! First the captain of The Kelly-Ann and his daughter, and then a boy only two years younger than her when she...

Joey hastened through the nearest doorway and wove her way through the maze of passageways to her four-berth cabin that she shared with Katie and Switch. She kept her expression as normal as possible.

The minute she reached the compact room she shared with the only other women on board, she entered the tiny bathroom, locked the door and sank to the floor shaking like a leaf.

"God, it's happening again. It's been four years and right now it feels like it was yesterday." She fought to keep her breathing under control and tears at bay. "Please, help me to deal with this without letting the captain or the crew down? Help me to be able to do my job properly?"

A soothing presence Joey had come to recognise since the day she had given Him her heart almost three years ago, stilled the fear within her. She was not alone. Words she knew so well from quoting them during sleepless nights, haunted by fear and the memory of an ordeal that had turned her life upside down, now sprang to mind. She gave voice to them and found comfort and strength to face the day ahead.

"He that dwells in the secret place of the most High shall abide under the shadow of the Almighty. I will say of the Lord, He is my refuge and my fortress: my God; in him will I trust."

Joey sighed and felt the tension leave her body. "Thank You, God. Thank You." She waited another minute in silence, allowing God's peace to wash over her. Finally with a calming breath, she rose and headed at an even pace to find Lon. It was time to get organised for the investigation on Lila Island.

~

Charlie crouched behind a thick tree trunk ensnared in vines. Dense green foliage hid her from view of the shack built into the hillside. She had made it to the cove from which the boat had sailed, only to find it void of human life. She had then followed a set of footprints still in the sand into dense jungle.

Now here she was studying a small sturdy dwelling nestled snugly into a steep hillside, partially covered with leaves and vines. What if her father was in there being held against his will? Had all of the pirates left or were some of them in the vicinity? Were they inside that hut?

"Only one way to find out." She crept through the undergrowth, keeping herself low to the ground. Her eyes warily scanned the forest around her. Birds continued to sing in the trees above, and in the distance she could hear the steady rhythm of waves upon the shore.

Perhaps they had left and taken her father with them? She drew to within one metre of the shack, listening intently for any sign of life. Nothing. She gently eased open the ancient wooden door. Rusty hinges protested loudly and she cringed, ceasing all movement.

Birds in the treetops stopped singing. She hoped it was because they were wondering what the crazy girl near the shack was up to, and not because she had unwanted company. Her heart pounded so fiercely she feared someone might hear.

Taking a silent shallow breath, she eased the door open further. The hinges groaned and she rolled her eyes.

Some cat burglar you'd make!

She peered inside. The light spilling in from the doorway made a small, rough-hewn table against the wall to her left visible. An upturned crate serving as a chair was tucked beneath it. Her eyes slowly adjusted to the darkness and she saw the shack consisted of only one room.

A bed sat against the right wall, not far from the table. Her heart nearly leapt clear out of her chest when she realised it was occupied.

With a quick glance behind her, she stepped inside. Thankfully the floor was made of dirt and could not creak with her weight. She slunk on silent toes to the foot of the bed and squinted to see the form sprawled upon it. Whoever it was, it wasn't her father. The figure was too lean and tall and he was wearing dress shoes, classy black slacks and a white dinner shirt.

Charlie studied the motionless man, half afraid he would leap up and grab her at any minute. Hang on!

She moved to the side of the bed and noticed with alarm that his hands were tied to the rusty iron bed head. Whoever he was, he was being held captive. And his face... there was no sign of stubble at all. This wasn't a man, it was a teenage boy.

She glanced warily behind her, knowing that whoever had left him here would soon return. Somehow she had to get him out of here. And why wasn't he moving? Was he dead? She reached out a tentative hand and shook his shoulder. Nothing. Charlie felt for a pulse in his neck beneath his jaw.

She picked up a steady beat. Well, he certainly wasn't dead. Perhaps he was a heavy sleeper?

Her gaze roamed the room one more time in the hopes of finding something that might give her a clue as to what was going on. Her eyes landed upon the table where partial light from the open doorway illuminated one corner. A small bottle caught the sunshine. It only took one stride from the bedside to reach the bottle.

She assessed it and concluded that it could be anything from a drug to a herbal remedy. She sat it back on the table and her fingers knocked something in the shadows nearby. She felt around carefully and her hand rested upon a plastic cylinder. Charlie lifted it into the light and her eyes widened in horror. It was a syringe.

Her gaze swung to the boy on the bed. So he had been drugged! That's what was in the bottle! Her sense of urgency tripled and she whipped out her multi-tool. Careful not to nick his hands, she hastily cut the ropes binding them soundly to the bed.

He groaned but did not stir. She debated her next move. She was tall but was she strong enough to carry him? She bit her lower lip. What other options did she have at this point? Whoever was holding this kid hostage would be back soon. She had to get him out now!

Charlie lifted a limp arm and pulled him to a sitting position. She drove her shoulder into his midsection, still holding his wrist firmly in her left hand, and hauled him up and over in the fireman's lift. She stumbled for a moment under his dead weight, and using every ounce of strength she possessed, she straightened and started for the door.

Once outside, she scanned the area. The terrain she had crossed today was steep. There was no way she could carry him to the place she had stayed the night before. She momentarily considered walking along the beach but quickly dismissed the idea. They would be too visible when the boy's captor returned by boat, and there was also the threat of the pirates.

Charlie had a hunch that they had nothing to do with this kidnapping. They were brutes who preferred automatic weapons. They were not sophisticated enough to sedate their hostages with drugs. Now she had another predator to be on the lookout for.

"Just Great! This island is bad luck!"

She walked toward the beach. Perhaps she could travel within the trees along the shore just out of sight? It would take longer and possibly be more dangerous, but there weren't a whole lot of other choices.

She pushed through dense foliage, carefully avoiding protruding roots lest she trip and fall. Finally the smell of the ocean greeted her senses and she spotted its azure depths through the trees.

Keeping their trunks entangled with vines between her and the sandy shore, Charlie started out with her heavy bundle in the direction she had come. Hopefully toward safety.

9

The hair on the back of Joey's neck suddenly stood on end and a chill ran down her spine. She had the odd sensation that she was being watched. Her alert gaze scanned the crowded tavern again. Her eyes skimmed over faces young and old, all sitting around enjoying a midmorning drink and a social chat. Why they all weren't out fishing or pearl hunting she had no idea.

A familiar face brought her wide-eyed gaze back for a second look, but he wasn't there. Had she been seeing things? She mentally shook herself. It was just fear and memories playing tricks on her mind. The room was packed. It could have been anyone.

She returned her attention to the bartender who was talking with Lieutenant Donnelly and Ollie. Woody was standing nearby and she inched closer to him. This place gave her the creeps. But then, with the news of Rylie Hunter's kidnapping, everything and everyone today gave her the creeps.

"There are some men who come in here off and on that fit your description," the bartender answered. "Especially the one with a scar down his face."

The man wore jeans, a flannel shirt and an apron that had been badly stained. His beard was unkempt, but his clear brown eyes above it were open and honest enough. He was Caucasian and probably originally from the Australian mainland. He talked as he dried freshly washed beer glasses.

55

"I don't know where they come from or where they go. They keep to themselves and don't cause any trouble." His face was thoughtful for a moment. "You might try asking down at the dock."

Lieutenant Donnelly smiled politely. "Thanks for your help."

"Sure thing."

The Lieutenant turned to his men and nodded toward the door. "Let's go." He led the way, weaving between tables in the crowded room. Ollie followed close behind and Joey stuck by Woody, impatient to get out of there.

She did not even register a negative remark about Asians grumbled under the breath of a patron they passed. She absently wondered who they were talking about. However, both Ollie and Woody stopped and turned. Woody's affront-ed gaze zeroed in on the rough fisherman who had made the comment. Ollie glared at the miscreant also. Both Joey and the Lieutenant halted and looked at the two seamen, but only Joey was wondering what was amiss.

"Watch your mouth, sailor," Ollie warned the man, a dan-gerous edge to his tone.

The unsavoury character snorted and smirked, leaning back in his chair haughtily. Woody's temper flared and he took a step toward him.

"Seaman Underwood," the Lieutenant's stern voice stopped him. "Fall in."

Woody passed the fisherman one last glare before he turned and followed the executive officer. Ollie put a hand on Joey's shoulder and protectively guided her out. She frowned in bewilderment. Why were they so upset?

The Lieutenant stopped outside the tavern and faced

them. "I know what he said was insulting, but you represent the Australian Navy, and the navy doesn't go beating up people for a prejudiced remark."

Joey looked between the men surrounding her, all of whom towered above her. Woody's jaw tensed and Ollie looked suitably chastised.

"What did the guy say?"

The lieutenant's kind gaze met hers. "He made a nasty remark regarding Asian people."

Joey's brows rose in surprise. "I didn't see anyone in there who was Asian."

Lieutenant Donnelly reined in a smile and dropped his gaze. Woody snorted, his eyes suddenly dancing with merriment. Ollie grinned. For some reason Joey couldn't fathom, they each found her remark highly entertaining.

She felt a little miffed at being on the outside of their joke. "What's so funny?"

The lieutenant's expression was kind, but his eyes gleamed with humour. "Joey, where are you from?"

She shrugged. "Cairns."

"Before that," he persisted gently.

"New South Wales. Why?" Her eyes suddenly widened with realisation and then darkened with anger. "Why that no good-" She caught herself before she could say something unpleasant. "He was talking about me, wasn't he?"

Ollie and Woody burst into laughter at her expense and the executive officer chuckled.

He grinned and started toward the dock. "Joey, you're a real character, you know that?"

"Wow she was slow on the uptake." Woody nudged her as they followed the lieutenant.

"She can't help it. She's an Aussie through and through." Ollie tugged her ponytail. "Don't let those gorgeous half moon eyes or that straight black hair fool ya."

Joey reluctantly smiled at their affectionate banter and gave Ollie a playful shove. She clipped Woody over the ear.

He grinned at her incorrigibly. "You hit like a girl."

"Maybe because I am one." She strolled briskly ahead.

~

Zacutti watched the four naval personnel walk toward the dock from his place at the tavern window. She had almost spotted him. The move of pretending to drop his wallet and ducking under the table to pick it up had saved his skin.

He studied her as she playfully shoved one of the tall men at her side. Yes, it was her alright. If she saw him it would end this whole operation and more than likely land him in prison, or at the very least on the outs with his boss. That meant no more money coming in and he wasn't about to let that happen.

His malicious eyes narrowed. He would have to deal with her permanently once and for all. How to go about that when she was surrounded by powerful, not to mention armed, navy sailors would be difficult. But then he had always been up for a good challenge.

~

Ezekiel ended the call on his mobile phone and dropped it onto the carpet. He was sitting on the sofa in their five star room at the resort, his elbows on his knees and his head cradled in his hands. His wife was perched on the edge of the king sized bed watching him.

He had spent every waking moment of the last two days searching for their son, to no avail. He seriously needed sleep. She worried over him just as much as she did Rylie.

"Who was it?" She sensed yet another burden now resting on his exhausted shoulders.

He looked up at her through despairing eyes and then dropped his gaze. "The Kelly-Ann was hijacked New Year's Day. Dave Mickleson and his daughter were taken hostage. The pirates have demanded a ransom the company simply can't afford." He blinked back tears and drew a deep breath.

Elizabeth's eyes widened and she stood. She crossed the plush carpet to kneel at his feet. "Was anyone hurt?"

"No. Liz, they found drugs on board and the federal police are treating me as a suspect."

"Surely you're joking!"

"I wish I was."

She frowned. "Why are we only just hearing about this now?"

Ezekiel sighed and rose. He moved to the large window overlooking Crystal Bay, a name befitting the beautiful harbour. "My executive, Ian Rochester, has been trying to contact me for days."

Understanding lit Elizabeth's sad blue eyes. He had been too busy searching for Rylie to check his messages from work. "So what do we do?"

He held out his arm in silent invitation and she joined him at the window, finding comfort in his embrace. "We pray for a miracle."

Her gaze turned from the sparkling water outside to her husband. "Just as well our God is in the business of miracles."

He smiled down at her, appreciation for her in his eyes. Elizabeth knew him well and could read the direction of his thoughts. She had a steadfast faith born of a rough start in life, something that he had expressed gratefulness for on more than one occasion.

She was familiar with his story. He had been raised by a wealthy family who lacked for nothing. He had worked for his father and finally the shipping business had been passed down to him when the older man retired. Ezekiel's personal faith had grown from a sense of emptiness. He'd had everything and yet it had never been fully satisfying. A friend had introduced him as a young man to Jesus Christ who had filled that void. And then Elizabeth had come along, not a penny to her name, but as he'd told her many times before, he'd thought her very beautiful and admired her love for God.

His family had objected at first, but she had won her way into their hearts with time. Their shared faith had been strengthened by her recent battle with cancer, and then she had been given a clean bill of health.

They had thought the worst was behind them, but now it seemed everything was on the line. Their son, Ezekiel's employee's lives, his business and his reputation. Yes, it would certainly take a God of miracles to get them out of this mess.

They bowed their heads and joined their hearts in prayer.

~

Charlie gently put her bundle down and dropped to the ground beside him, panting from exertion. He was still out of it. Whatever his captor had given him was mighty strong stuff.

She estimated that she had come at least two or three kilometres from the shack. She wasn't far enough away to feel safe, and yet looking at the sky filling quickly with black churning clouds, she figured it would have to do. A nasty tropical storm was brewing, and remembering the stories her father had told her about those, she wanted to take cover as soon as possible.

After catching her breath, she stood and studied the area around her. Ahead was the beach, the waves already white with foam from a strong wind that would soon be classified gale force. To her right and left the treetops swayed and leaves rustled loudly. Behind her was an incline. She decided to scout for shelter in that direction. Checking that the boy was okay, she started further inland on her own.

Fifteen minutes of fighting her way through dense foliage produced the base of a mountain, one among many on this wild island. Thick jungle covered it like a cloak, yet boulders abounded upon its rugged slopes. Charlie was thrilled to find a large overhang that would prove adequate shelter during the coming storm.

She hastened back to the drugged teenager, hoisted him over her shoulder again and staggered to the overhang. If she pushed herself to her limit, they might make it before the storm set in.

10

"Well men," Commander Kelly conferred with his crew below decks. "We've been informed by the mainland that a cyclone is in the area. It's predicted to hit the other side of the Pearl Island coastline in the early morning hours.

"We'll stay in port tonight. The cove will provide us with shelter from the brunt of the weather. There's nothing for us to do but sit tight until tomorrow morning when it's expected to blow over."

Jaffa's eyes lit with a hopeful gleam. "Does that mean what I think it does, Captain?"

Commander Kelly smiled in amusement. "Yes, Leading Seaman Williams, it does. Tonight's watch is still scheduled, however those not on watch are free to go ashore for the evening after the ship is secured." His countenance became suddenly stern. "Make sure you're all back on board by twenty-two hundred hours. The storm won't have arrived by then, but I want to make certain you're all safe and sound below deck when it does.

"Like I said, we should be well protected on this side of the island, but I don't believe in taking unnecessary risks. He turned to address Joey and Coz, a twinkle in his green eyes. "Galley crew, you'll be pleased to have the night off."

Joey grinned and answered with a hearty, "Yes sir."

Commander Kelly smiled broadly. "Enjoy your evening sailors. Be sensible and stick together. Dismissed."

Several cheers and whoops of delight accompanied the captain's dismissal. Sailors wandered to their quarters to prepare for an evening on the town. Joey accompanied Switch and Katie to their shared room where they changed into civilian attire.

"I like that red dress," Switch remarked with a smile at Joey.

Joey zipped up a comfortable knee length, fitted garment. "That colour suits you."

The chef smiled appreciatively. "Thanks. What are your plans for tonight?"

"Just a few drinks with the boys and maybe a game or two of pool. You?"

Joey shrugged. What she really wanted to do was go to church, but it was Friday and none would be open. That was one bad thing about the navy. So much of her time was spent at sea or in training.

"Having someone else cook for me will be excitement enough."

Katie chuckled. She and Switch were ready ahead of her and made their way to the deck where the boys were gathering.

After a rummage through her things, Joey finally found a red pair of sandals, slipped them on and strode into the hallway. The majority of the crew was already on deck and the passageways were strangely quiet.

Darkness had not yet fallen, and yet in the belly of the ship where there were no windows, it was already dark. Florescent lights brightly lit the uppermost level, however down here small night lights produced an eerie red glow.

Uneasiness crept through the spooked cook. She passed

the junior sailors' quarters, all the while listening to the creaking and groaning of steel contracting as it slowly cooled after the day's heat. It was a freaky sound.

Suddenly a berth door crashed open behind her and an arm shot out and grabbed her around the neck and shoulders. Memories of that night four years ago flooded her mind and her heart leapt into her throat.

Joey reacted instantly, her right elbow jabbing backward into the assailant's stomach. In the next moment she dipped her left shoulder and flipped him over. He landed with a hard thump and a groan on the floor.

"Ow, Joey!" Coz rolled onto his stomach and then got to his knees.

Joey's shaking hand flew to her mouth and she suppressed a sob. "Cozzi, I'm so sorry!" She swallowed hard against the lump of terror in her throat.

The young man held both his midsection and the back of his head that had collided with the floor. He slowly got to his feet, fixing her with a glare.

"What'd you do that for? You nearly cracked my skull open!"

The frightened chef tried to control her rapid breathing. "I'm sorry, I didn't mean to-"

"Yes you did! I was gonna ask if you wanted a game of pool, but you can forget it." He scowled at her, looking highly offended.

She tried to apologise again, but he turned and stalked off, still rubbing the back of his head.

Joey sank to the floor, her back to the wall. Her heart pounded in her ears and the face from the tavern flashed before her mind's eye. Had it really been him or was she paranoid?

Lord, please forgive me? I hurt Coz.

Tears blurred her vision and she clenched her hands to stop them from shaking.

I'm so tired of being afraid and living on edge. Today isn't the first time I've gone into shock or had flashbacks. Please, give me closure?

She sat there for quite some time, gathering composure and the courage to leave the ship. This place had become her safe haven and the galley, her happy place. Now even there she felt uneasy. Perhaps she should try explaining her situation to Coz?

The sound of footsteps echoed loudly in the hallways and a masculine pair of legs clad in board shorts descended the stairs at the end of the passageway, followed by a broad chest in a loose light blue shirt. Joey sprang to her feet and met the executive officer's concerned gaze.

"Coz told me what happened."

Joey quickly brushed away tears with her fingers, but not before he noticed them.

"Are you alright?"

"He jumped out of nowhere and grabbed me from behind."

"He admitted that. You gave him a decent sized egg on his head."

Joey felt a sinking feeling in the pit of her stomach. She could be charged for what she'd done. Harming another sailor was a serious offence.

"He scared the life out of me." She hoped she did not have to go into why.

"I figured as much and told him he deserved what he got. I

know you two play rough sometimes, but he needs to know when he's gone too far."

Joey sighed with relief and looked at the lieutenant with renewed appreciation. He must have seen the relief in her eyes because he smiled.

"May I escort you ashore?" He made a theatrical sweep of his hand, indicating she was to precede him.

Her smile broadened at the sudden change in his demeanour. "Why of course, sir." She found her mood lightening with the mischievous twinkle in his lively eyes.

She dropped her mask of confidence for a moment as she climbed the stairs. "Has he forgiven me?"

He took the stairs two at a time behind her, eager to get ashore. "He's still put out. Just give him a little time to get over his wounded pride and I'm sure he'll come around."

~

Coz directed several sharp comments Joey's way as the crew wandered into the small harbour town of Abbotsford. The boys found this highly amusing, however Joey was deeply upset. She could understand his cold treatment, although part of her agreed with the XO. Coz had gone too far and should have expected such a reaction from a woman alone who knew there were pirates in the area.

They arrived at a small hotel further into the small settlement that appeared to be quite a few notches above the tavern in class. Katie and Switch quickly claimed the pool table, while the boys went straight for the bar.

Meanwhile, Joey chose the cosy restaurant in the adjoining room. Lieutenant Donnelly must have seen her downcast expression and took pity on her.

"Mind if join you? I'm starved and a drink just won't cut it."

Joey's smile was friendly, but not as bright as usual. "That's fine, just as long as you don't mind me scoffing my food down like a hungry miner."

The lieutenant chuckled. "Not at all. I reserve the right to use my fingers whenever I please. That okay with you?"

Joey's smile broadened. She appreciated the knack he had for lifting her mood at a moment's notice. She was already beginning to feel like herself again.

"Deal."

She perused the menu and made a quick selection. She was able then to sit back and study the man opposite her, who seemed to take forever to make up his mind. His face was a study in concentration. Her eyes sparkled with mischief.

"Just as well, sir, that you don't give orders at the same rate it takes you to choose a meal."

His clear blue gaze met hers. "I only get to eat three times a day and I like to make each meal count." There was a hint of humour in his tone. "And by the way, we're off duty. You can call me Josh."

"Then I guess you can call me Joey," she quipped with a straight face.

His eyes gleamed with amusement. "I always call you Joey."

She rolled her eyes and muttered under her breath, "Officers, they think they're a cut above us all!"

Joshua laughed and sat his menu aside. "Alright, I've decided."

"What will it be tonight?"

"Lasagne. No wait, I think I'll have the seafood pasta. But then the pizza looks good too." He appeared to mentally seesaw for another moment until he caught the merry twinkle in the velvety brown eyes watching him from across the table. With a sheepish grin, he settled back in his chair.

"I'll live dangerously and just say whatever comes to mind when the waiter arrives."

"That'll be kind of hard for your obsessive compulsive personality. Are you sure you can handle it?"

Joshua reined in a smile, clearly unwilling to encourage her and receive more teasing.

"So, Joey, where were you originally from, other than Cairns and New South Wales?"

That impish light remained in her eyes and she could not resist. "I lived in Melbourne for a while when I was a kid."

He levelled her with a look. "I meant where did-"

"I know what you meant." Joey chuckled and smiled. "I was adopted as a baby from Taiwan by a wealthy Australian couple."

The lieutenant's brows rose in interest. "What do they do?"

Joey hesitated for a moment. Would he make the connection? Hardly likely. "He was in the shipping industry, but enough about me. What about you? Why doesn't a homely sailor like yourself have a family? Surely some girl out there has taken pity on you?"

Joshua smiled, thoroughly enjoying her company. "One did when I was young."

"Yeah, you're really old now," she remarked dryly, guessing him to be in his early thirties.

He chuckled and continued. "We were married when I was

twenty-one. Her name was Amanda."

Compassion entered Joey's eyes. "Was?"

Joshua's smile was kind, but behind it she read pain. "She died in a car accident six years ago. She was five months pregnant at the time. They tried to save the baby, but he was just too small."

"What a terrible thing to go through."

In a way, she had lost her family too, and she could certainly understand grief, even if she hadn't lost a family member. "I'm sorry I teased you about it."

"You didn't know," he answered graciously.

The waiter arrived. They ordered their meals and the conversation flowed onto lighter subjects. By the time they had devoured their food, they were laughing again and swapping funny stories of life on board a navy ship. Laughter was coming from the bar as well.

"It sounds like they're having fun out there. Want to go see what they're up to?"

"Sure. I could go a pint of apple cider," she quipped and waggled her brows.

Joshua grinned. "Me too."

They wandered together into the adjoining room. A pool table stood over near a large window overlooking the bay, which was no longer visible because darkness had fallen. Booths lined the wall onto which the door opened and several tables were set out in the remaining space. The booths and tables were occupied by the crew of the Hartfield, several of whom appeared to have had a few drinks too many.

Wilko spotted the XO and waved him and Joey over to the bar against the wall opposite the entrance, where he was sitting with Ollie. They sat down and ordered drinks, the lieutenant a coke and Joey apple cider.

The cook's eyes searched the room for Coz. He was playing pool with Farmer. She sighed with relief. At least he wasn't drinking it up with Jaffa and Woody. They must have emptied their glasses because they got up from their booth and wove their way between tables to the bar.

"Lieutenant, where've ya bin?" Jaffa clapped him soundly on the back. "We've been havin' a great time in here."

Joshua cringed slightly from the pungent odour of alcohol on Jaffa's breath. "I've been enjoying civilised company over a tasty meal."

Woody frowned. "Sounds kind of boring if you ask me."

The lieutenant smiled in amusement. "I'll take boring any day over the headache you'll have tomorrow. Go easy on the sauce, boys. You're on duty early in the morning."

Joey's gaze remained upon Coz. She hated the tension hanging between them. "Excuse me a minute." She got down from her stool. The men continued to talk while she wandered over to the pool table.

Farmer glanced up from the game in front of him and smiled a welcome. "G'day Joey. You any good at pool? Coz here is whipping my sorry tail."

She smiled in return. "Sorry, nobody can beat Cozzi, least of all me."

The young man in question glanced up at her, his expression saying he was surprised at the compliment when he had given her the cold shoulder earlier that evening.

"Coz, I didn't mean to hurt you before. You scared the life out of me and I just reacted. I hope you'll forgive me."

Petty Officer Farmer discreetly took an acute interest in chalking his pool cue while Coz calmly made his shot. Joey was wondering if he would even acknowledge her, when he finally straightened and looked her in the eye.

"It's going to cost you donuts," he said with a deadpan.

Joey's gaze narrowed. "Iced or sugared?"

"Iced of course." A smile tugged at the corners of his mouth.

"It's a deal if you do the dishes afterward."

He grinned. "Done."

The apprehensive knot inside Joey's stomach loosened and she relaxed. "Thanks Coz."

"Yeah, I'm sorry I scared you. I guess this pirate thing has us all a bit jumpy."

Something niggled in the back of Joey's mind. One day she would have to tell him about her past, but not yet, not until she had a handle on it. "I'll leave you to your game guys."

Farmer lifted a hand in a casual wave as did Coz and she went back to the bar. Jaffa and Woody now occupied the place beside her stool and on her left Wilko, Ollie and the lieutenant were discussing and comparing mechanical and technical differences between the Armidale class patrol boat and its predecessor the Fremantle class.

Joey tuned out. The Armidale got them where they had to go and that was all she cared about. Whether it was fifteen metres longer or eighty-five tons heavier with stabilizers, she didn't care.

She took a sip of her cider and frowned at the odd taste. Jaffa and Woody snickered beside her and she glanced up at them in alarm.

A horrible sick feeling churned in her stomach. "Did you spike my drink?"

"Is it a bit stronger than your usual brew?" Jaffa teased.

Her face drained completely of colour. They had violated her trust. Did they have any idea what could happen as a result of a spiked drink? That night from four years ago sprang to mind so vividly for the umpteenth time that day and Joey felt shock slowly steeling over her again.

Woody sobered quickly with her strange reaction. "Are you okay?"

Her left hand grasped the bar and her knuckles whitened. Wilko, Ollie and the Lieutenant heard the concerned tone in his voice and turned curiously to listen to the interchange beside them.

Joey snapped back to the present and stared at her shipmates with a mixture of fear and anger. "Don't you ever take away my power to choose!"

Woody laid a hand on her arm. "I'm sorry Joey. We just thought-"

"Don't touch me!" She stepped away and swallowed the fear clawing at her throat as memories played one after the other across the stage of her mind. She mentally shook herself, fighting to suppress them.

"Hey Joey, what's the matter?" Joshua too looked concerned.

She could feel that she was pale and her hands were shaking. Her breathing was becoming uneven, despite her efforts to control it.

Joshua got down from his stool and she automatically backed away. She desperately wanted to be back aboard the Hartfield safe in her bunk. She turned and strode toward the door, running the second her feet left the building.

~

The lieutenant didn't hesitate for a second. He walked to the door so as not to draw attention, and Ollie saw him run after her as soon as the door closed behind him. He glared at Woody and Jaffa.

"What did you do?"

Jaffa shrugged. "It was just a joke."

"You spiked her drink, didn't you?" Wilko guessed, an unhappy crease appearing between his brows.

Woody looked ashamed, while Jaffa seemed bent on maintaining his pride.

"How were we to know she'd flip her lid?"

Ollie got stuck into him. "Did it ever occur to you two buffoons that she doesn't drink alcohol for a reason?"

Jaffa snorted. "What reason could that be?"

Having witnessed her reaction, he could make a pretty good guess as to why. "That someone might have done that to her in the past and taken advantage of her you nitwit." He got down from his stool, intending to go after Joey as well.

Wilko put a hand on his shoulder. "She'll be alright, Ollie. The XO will take her back to the ship."

Ollie was reluctant to stay, and yet when he thought of how kind the second in command was, he relaxed. Joey was in safe hands. Woody held up a red wallet on the counter.

"She left this behind."

"Then you'd better give it to her when you apologise later," Wilko replied sharply.

Woody slumped at the counter and leant on his fist. Jaffa was quiet also, Ollie's observation having sunk into his awareness. Both appeared to have a troubled conscience.

11

Joey was out of breath and beginning to see spots dance across her vision. Was she even running in the right direction? Her heart felt like a cold stone in her chest and she was shaking all over. If she didn't stop and catch her breath, she would pass out.

She sank onto the front steps of a small chapel at the edge of the village, drew her knees up to her chest and rested her head on them.

"God help me? The past is breathing down my neck and I think I'm losing my mind!" A sob escaped her lips and then another. How long had it been since she had really cried?

She shed a few tears every now and then, but never about what had happened. It haunted her dreams and at times her waking moments, yet she had always pushed it deeper inside, never knowing just what to do with the horror and the hurt. Tears simply weren't enough.

No child, you're not losing your mind, the gentle impression nudged into her thoughts. *You're finally facing what happened.*

His reassurance penetrated the darkness in her soul with a ray of hope. "Really God?"

Really.

She sighed and her breathing slowly evened out. The tears kept coming and would not stop, like a dam that had burst its walls. The images, the icy cold sensation of the needle sliding into her, the memories, the frustration and the fear. It all came rushing back as vivid as the day it occurred.

A large hand gently smoothed her hair and she nearly leapt out of her skin, bumping hard into the closed chapel door behind her.

Joshua withdrew his hand sharply, clearly startled by her response and the fear etched into every feature.

"It's okay Joey, it's me. I'm not going to hurt you."

"Lieutenant." She choked back terror and fought to calm her breathing again. Still the tears would not stop.

In slow deliberate movements, he sat on the step beside her. The soft ding of a bell in the distance was whipped along by the same wind that blew long dark wisps of hair across Joey's face.

The storm hadn't hit yet but it was obviously on its way. No wonder the tavern had been full of sailors. No one in their right mind would be caught on the open ocean on a night like this.

The sound of waves hurling themselves against the beach carried through the disquieted darkness. The only light to throw off its heavy cloak was that which spilled from village homes and the occasional bar. The air now held a distinct bite.

"Come inside." The lieutenant rose to open the chapel door. It was not locked, so he stepped inside the small, old-fashioned wooden structure.

Joey reluctantly followed. He found a pew in the back row and patted the empty space beside him. She hesitated distrustfully for a moment and then edged forward and sat.

It took all of her powers of reason not to flee, reminding herself over and over again of the kind and caring person that he was.

"This is not about pirates being in the area and it's not about Jaffa and Woody," he began calmly, his astute gaze studying her in what little light the window caught from nearby houses and tossed inside the small wooden church. "What's going on Joey?"

"I don't think I can talk about it." Her quaking voice was thick with emotion. The memories kept coming. She just wanted it all to go away.

She wished she could return to the carefree teenager she had been, the one who freely trusted and knew that the world was a beautiful place full of opportunity. The girl who revelled in dark nights because they gave her a clearer view of the stars. The young woman who had felt secure in a loving family and freely shared her true self, able to connect with others, understanding that they were like her and she was like them.

But that girl was gone, her innocence robbed, her trust violated, her ideals shattered. The world was full of darkness and that darkness had scarred her deeply.

"I think you should. I don't know what you've been through that's causing you so much fear and pain, but I do understand grief, and the only way to deal with it is to let it surface."

The conviction in Joshua's voice caught her attention. He leaned forward and rested his elbows on his knees, patiently waiting. A full five minutes of silence passed and finally in a ragged voice she began to tell her story.

"My real name is Jessica Hyndman."

Lieutenant Donnelly raised his brows in surprise and turned in the pew to look at her fully. He did not interrupt.

"On the night of my high school graduation, I went out with some friends to a club. I didn't know it then, but they spiked my drink. It tasted strange but I drank it all. I wasn't used to alcohol so I was more than a little drunk.

"I went outside in the fresh air hoping to clear my head. I didn't even hear him." Joey shook her head and swallowed hard against the lump in her throat. "A huge arm grabbed me from behind and something sharp jabbed into my side. He tossed me over his shoulder and carried me away. I fought at first, but within minutes I couldn't move. From there it's hazy."

She frowned into the chapel interior, seeing only the fuzzy images of that night passing before her eyes.

"I have a vague recollection of being in a car boot, then tied to a bed. I could see and hear and feel everything around me, but it was like it was all from a different world. He didn't harm me or hit me, but every time the drugs were wearing off, I would feel the needle go into my arm again, taking away my choice, my freedom."

"You were kidnapped?" Joshua looked horrified.

"The police found me five days later, heavily drugged, starved and dehydrated, but otherwise unharmed. The kidnapper got away. We all thought it was over. And then a few nights later our dog went crazy outside barking up a storm. Dad found large boot imprints in the garden soil outside my window.

"The police refused requests to put me in protective custody, offering other solutions like hi tech alarm systems for the house. Knowing that wouldn't be enough and that he would be back, my dad drove me interstate, changed my name and took me to enlist in the navy. He figured I'd be safer surrounded by navy personnel on a boat out in the ocean.

"He gave me a large sum of cash and said goodbye. He told me not to contact them in any way until he got word to me that the kidnapper had been found. That was four years ago."

"I don't understand. Why would your dad cut off contact?" Joshua was trying to fathom what would drive a loving father to take such a drastic step. Joey understood the struggle. By the look in his eyes, she guessed that if his son had lived, there was no way he would let the boy out of his sight given a situation like hers occurred. She looked at the lieutenant with a depth of sadness one might drown in.

"He believed my kidnapping had something to do with him. He didn't know who was trying to get at him or why, so he figured I'd have a better chance of staying safe if I was removed from his life."

The separation was still painful, but she had come to grips with it and her reason told her that he had been correct. However her heart still disagreed.

"And you haven't heard from him since?"

Joey shook her head.

"Was it Rylie Hunter's kidnapping that brought all of this to the surface?"

"I suppose. What really got me spooked was the tavern today. For one split second I thought I saw his face in the crowd." She felt a little foolish for her paranoia.

"Whose? The boy's?" Joshua's eyes widened with realisation. "You meant the kidnapper's."

Joey nodded. "This whole mess has got me tangled in knots. I'm sorry I freaked out back there."

The lieutenant frowned as he pondered her revelation.

"You had every right to. What I'm more worried about is if it really was him."

A chill ran down her spine. "You don't think it could be, do you? I figured it was just paranoia."

"Maybe it is memories that are toying with reality, or maybe it was him. Either way, I'd feel a whole lot better if you were on the Hartfield right now. Come on, let's get you to the ship." He rose. "It's been a big night and I'm sure you're exhausted."

"Josh?" She looked up at him, finding her appreciation deepening to affection.

"Yeah?"

"Thanks for listening. I've never been able to speak about it before. My parents were so upset that I couldn't give them the details, and then I was forced into silence to protect my identity."

She stood and he placed a reassuring hand on her shoulder, gently stroking her with his thumb. The kind gesture touched a lonely place in her soul.

"You can talk to me anytime. I hope you don't mind," he said as he guided her through the doorway, "but I'd like you to tell the captain about it too. Aside from the fact he needs to know in order to assure your safety, he should be made aware that you might have seen the kidnapper today. And you never know, maybe it's the same guy and he had something to do with the boy's disappearance."

Joshua closed the chapel door behind them and strode with her down to the large pier where several fishing vessels, as well as the HMAS Hartfield, were docked.

"I guess it's possible." She dreaded the prospect of going over it all in detail again. Maybe the lieutenant was right?

Perhaps the best way of dealing with this once and for all was to face it head on?

~

Joey watched the lieutenant's retreating back as he strode down the pier toward the village. He had kindly walked her to the ship and then excused himself to go let the men know that the weather was picking up and they would need to return a little earlier. She was standing at the top of the gang-way and turned now to head inside. She then froze.

My purse!

Joey rolled her eyes in exasperation. She had left it on the counter back at the bar. She could hope that one of the boys would bring it back with them, but it was unlikely. They might not even know it was hers. She turned again to the gangway, debating what to do.

The lieutenant was already striding up the incline toward the village. There was no way he would hear her if she called his name, he was too far away. She could jog and catch up with him.

Something niggled in the back of her mind. Was it fear or wisdom? She wasn't sure. There seemed to be an awful lot of darkness between where he was and where she now stood. She inwardly scolded herself for being a coward and jogged down the gangway onto the pier, deciding she would run to catch up. The dock was not overly long, only fifty or so metres.

In an easy flowing gait, she trotted its full length. Her feet touched the island and a dark shadow charged from behind. The solid figure tackled her to the ground and before she could even let out a startled scream, a large hand clamped over her mouth and something sharp jabbed her in the side. She tried to cry for help but all that came forth was a muted sound.

She kicked and fought against the weight of a stocky body pinning her to the ground, but he was too strong and her limbs were fast losing strength. Her mind screamed that this could not be happening again and rage flooded her that her will and her freedom had been taken away.

Within minutes, reality around her melded into a strange nightmare. She could think, see and feel, and yet it was like being in a dream world. She was conscious but unable to move. Her brain shouted for her arms and legs to fight, however the message could not reach them and they remained limp.

She was tossed over a beefy shoulder and carried back onto the pier. Joey was vaguely aware of her captor stepping onto a rocking surface and descending with her into the depths of what had to be a boat. She was dropped haphazardly onto a soft surface.

Her now blurred vision saw the dark figure climb a ladder and disappear from sight. A second later there was a loud bang and a hatch closed off the last shaft of light in her nonsensical world.

Part of her raged with frustration and the other drifted aimlessly like a boat bobbing upon the ocean.

12

Rain pelted down in a violent torrent and cyclonic wind lashed at the overhang as though it had a personal vendetta against the two teenagers sheltering there. Thankfully the overhang was deep enough to protect them from the worst of the storm. However, the rain still managed to soak them to the bone.

Charlie shivered and huddled against the rock wall behind her. The boy lay at her side, semi conscious by the looks of him. He had curled into a ball and now stared with a vague expression at the rain blowing in around him. She wondered what he must be thinking. Did he understand where he was and that he had been rescued? Was he afraid or still too drugged to know what was going on?

Her mind turned to her father. Was he alright? Had they ransomed him as they had planned, or was he still being held hostage? Did he know she was alive? And what of her mother? By now she would know what had happened. How was she coping?

Charlie desperately wished she could somehow get in contact with her. But that was just not possible, unless she could find the pirates' base and swipe some of their equipment.

A slow smile spread across her pale, icy cold face. Now there was a cunning idea! Yes, that was what she would do. As soon as the boy could travel, they would set out in search of the pirates' hideout, and with a little luck, use their equipment against them.

~

Woody obeyed his jangling conscience and knocked on the female junior sailors' door, Joey's purse in hand. Jaffa, it appeared, was lacking the courage to apologise face to face, even though it was clear he felt as bad as his accomplice did.

They had come back with the rest of the crew, after the executive officer returned from seeing Joey to the ship and ordered them all aboard due to the escalating weather. It was almost ten pm now.

There was shuffling behind the portal and then it opened wide. Switch stood in the doorway in a yellow tank top and shorts. Her short brown hair, which was usually spiked, had been freshly washed and her brown eyes looked a little sleepy. Behind her, Katie was already in her rack, a book in hand.

"What's up Woody?" Switch looked curious over his late night visit.

"Can I talk to Joey for a minute?"

"I'm sorry. She's not in yet."

His shoulders sagged in disappointment.

"I can tell her you want to see her when she gets back."

"Alright, that'd be-" He broke off mid sentence when he realised what she had said. "What do you mean she's not in? The XO walked her back himself before he came to get us."

Switch shrugged. "I meant she's not in here with us. She'll be on board somewhere."

"Oh, I guess I'll check the galley. If I miss her and she goes to bed, tell her I said I'm sorry, and would you please give her this?" He handed Switch the red purse.

The young woman frowned in intrigue and took it. The curious expression on her face begged the question, what had he done to offend their easygoing cook?

"Sure. You could also try the sailor on watch. He'll have a record of who came on board and when."

"I'll do that."

Woody turned and strode down the passageway, his face troubled.

~

"What do you mean her name's not on the list?" Woody snatched the clipboard off Leading Seaman Ron Debartista, who was still on watch in the bridge. He scanned the list of names.

Upon their return ten minutes ago, each crewmember had reported their arrival. Twenty people were present and accounted for out of twenty-one. Joey's name was missing.

"Able Seaman Shafer isn't here. Hasn't she reported in yet?"

Ron shook his head and took back the clipboard. "Not yet. I was going to give her another ten minutes to show before alerting the officer on deck."

Woody frowned in confusion. "Didn't you see her come aboard? The XO walked her back himself."

A shadow of anxiety passed across Ron's features. "No, but I did answer a few calls on the bridge. She could have come on board while I was talking and simply not checked in with me."

Woody was not convinced. "That's not procedure. She

knows that."

Ron rose from the radio operator's desk chair, now very uneasy. "Do you think something's happened to her?"

Woody rubbed the back of his neck and bit his lower lip, hesitant to share the shameful trick he and Jaffa had pulled on her. "No, but she was pretty upset earlier and... Never mind. I'll go check with the XO. He'll probably know where she is."

"Do that."

"'Night Ron," he offered distractedly and left the bridge in search of Lieutenant Donnelly.

~

"What do you mean Ron didn't see her return. I delivered her to the Hartfield myself and saw her walk up the gangway."

Joshua held the door to his berth open as he spoke with Seaman Underwood. Inside Lieutenant Shepparton was stretched out on his rack with a sketchpad and pencil in hand.

"Ron didn't see her return and she hasn't checked in with the first watch yet."

Joshua's heart rate increased and he pushed past Woody into the passageway. "And you're sure she's not on board?" He strode purposefully toward the captain's cabin.

Woody followed in his wake. "Nobody's seen her and she's not in her room. Do you think she left the ship after you dropped her off? She was pretty upset after what we did."

"No, I don't. She knew I was going to fetch all of you. True, she was shaken, but she was calm by the time I dropped her off. Besides," he commented over his shoulder as he knocked on the captain's door, "she's a smart girl. She wouldn't be caught out in this weather for quids."

The captain's door opened and he blinked several times to focus what appeared to be blurry eyes.

"Lieutenant, this had better be good. I haven't slept properly in three days."

"Sir, I believe Able Seaman Shafer is missing."

The gravity in his expression and the urgency in his tone cleared the last vestiges of sleep from Commander Kelly's face. The captain rubbed a hand through his ginger hair and stepped aside to allow his second in command to enter.

"I want details."

~

Rylie stirred and slowly opened his eyes. Everything was blurry. He blinked several times to clear his vision. A pair of light blue irises were staring back at him only inches away.

Adrenaline charged through his veins like an electrical current and he reacted instinctively. He thrust the figure leaning over him away and pulled himself upright. He scrambled backward until his back met with a rock wall.

"Hey! What was that for? I was just checking to see if you were still alive," a female voice scolded.

He squinted and she came into view. A tall girl, roughly his age, rose on her elbows from the place where she had fallen. She slowly sat up and brushed off mud from already dirty jeans, scowling at him.

He swallowed hard against the fear pumping through him. "Who are you?"

"I was about to ask you the same question."

His chest heaved with rapid breathing and his wide sea green eyes held alarm and distrust. "Where am I?"

"I've got no idea." Some of her annoyance drained. "I got you away from that shack if it's any comfort. You were kidnapped, right?"

His breathing gradually calmed and his eyes closed in relief. He swallowed the lump in his throat and blinked back tears. "Thank You, God!" A shudder ran down his tall, sturdy frame after his whispered thanks.

Charlie scoffed and half smiled. "It wasn't God who got you out of there, mate. You got a name?"

He looked at her uncertainly. "Rylie Hunter, and you?"

"Charlotte Mickleson. You can call me Charlie." She extended her hand and he hesitantly reached forward and shook it. After the official introduction, she sat facing him and crossed her legs. "So, how did you end up on this deserted island?"

Rylie pulled his legs to his chest defensively and wrapped his arms around them. "I don't know. I was at the Southern Star Restaurant when a guy grabbed me from behind and jabbed a needle in me. I think I was on a boat at one time but I don't remember getting here. Are we still on Pearl Island?"

Charlie's mouth flattened in a dry expression. "Not likely. My dad's ship was hijacked by pirates nearby and they took us hostage. I fell out of their zodiac and they thought I'd drowned so I managed to escape, but they've still got my dad. They're on this island somewhere. Did you see the guy's face, you know, the one that took you?"

The hair on the back of Rylie's neck stood on end and a shudder ran down his spine as the memory of a pair of emotionless brown eyes that gleamed amber in the light, sprang to mind. A black, scruffy beard covered his strong jaw line and just below his right eye on his cheekbone was a small tattoo of a skull. Rylie knew he would remember that face until the day he died.

"Yeah, I saw him."

"Where do you think he went? I saw a boat sail away from the cove where I found you." She puzzled over it for a moment. "But then you were kind of out of it. I'm guessing you haven't got a clue."

Rylie frowned in irritation. "He may have drugged me but I could still hear what was going on around me, even if it was a little vague."

Her expression said she did not like the fact he was annoyed with her. "Okay, then where did he go?"

He just wanted to be left alone. He needed time to process what he had been through and her questions were confronting. "What is this, a police interrogation?"

Charlie cast him a patronising glare. "Phew, who woke up on the wrong side of the rock this morning?" She got up and strode from the overhang into bright daylight.

It was hard to believe the weather had tried to kill them the night before. The air was balmy and the sky was cobalt blue. However, the storm had left its mark by damaging the trees closest to the coast. Roots had been exposed and branches were tangled with other fallen trees around them.

It had been miserable last night in the overhanging, but it had saved their lives.

13

Shep studied the equipment before him. "Sir, the radar is picking up a vessel to the northeast."

Commander Kelly glanced over his shoulder at the navigator from his place in the captain's chair. "How close?"

Lieutenant Donnelly hoped this was the boat they were tracking. He moved behind Shep to study the radar. A small, unidentified blip blinked on the screen.

"At top speed we'll rendezvous in half an hour, sir."

"Good. Increase speed to twenty-five knots and head straight for it. XO, prepare a boarding party and standby."

"Yes sir." Lieutenant Donnelly strode from the bridge to carry out the order. Joey's smiling face as she had teased him over dinner the night before flashed before his mind's eye, quickly followed by that same beautiful face touched by sorrow and fear later that evening.

It haunted him.

He should have taken her straight to the captain rather than leaving her on the deck. They had conducted a thorough search of the dock and found nothing. Then Lon had returned to the ship with a pair of red sandals that he had discovered partially covered by sand several metres beyond the pier.

The watchman gave a brief rundown on activity in the port, noting the odd occurrence of a commercial angling vessel sailing out of the cove just as the storm was arriving.

Having searched the island and come up empty, the captain had decided to pursue the boat.

It had been a rough night on a very angry ocean but the Armidale class ship, although pushed to its limit of Sea State nine, had weathered it well.

With daylight had come reprieve from the violent storm. Now the ocean was calm, reminding Joshua of a fickle woman; spitting mad one moment, docile and affectionate the next.

He headed straight for the galley, where he knew the crew would be having breakfast. Well, only those with cast iron stomachs unaffected by the pitching and rolling they had undergone the night before. He opened the door to the wardroom. Lon and Wilko were the only ones brave enough to face food.

"Lon, I've got orders to form a boarding party. We think we've found the boat we've been chasing. We'll only need one RHIB. I want Farmer, you and Wilko on board with me. You choose the other three men."

Ready for action, Lon stood and carried his bowl to the galley counter, brushing past the XO.

"Yes sir." He handed Coz his half eaten meal. "I'll take Woody, Ollie and Daz."

Coz, who was already beginning the morning cleanup, overheard the conversation. "I'll go."

Both Lon and Lieutenant Donnelly glanced at him in surprise. The XO's expression was understanding but grim.

"I know you're good mates with Joey, Coz, but this is the bosun's call," he replied kindly but with firmness.

Coz stared at Lon with fiery eyes. "I want to come. This is Joey we're talking about."

Lon weighed his decision. Joshua could understand the pros and cons. On one hand, Coz's emotional involvement could cause problems. On the other, it could prove a bonus. Nobody would be able to stand in the angry young man's way.

The corners of Lon's mouth twitched with a smile. Apparently he was thinking the same thing.

"Alright, but what I say goes. If you don't like it, then stay put in the galley."

"Yes sir." Coz removed his apron and prepared to follow.

Lieutenant Donnelly wanted the team in place quickly so they could move into action at a moment's notice. "Okay, let's brief the men and arm up."

~

Joey could feel her senses clearing and her strength slowly returning. She lifted an arm and rubbed her face. Her hands weren't tied. With that realisation, she forced herself to move. She had to get out of here before he returned.

She pulled herself into a sitting position and swung her legs over the side of a tacky cot. Her bare feet touched a wet wooden floor. Water rushed over her toes with the boat's gentle rocking motion.

Why was the room waterlogged? Perhaps she was in the lowest hold and there had been rough seas? Despite slightly blurred vision, she scanned the room. It was small and the only piece of furniture was the stale smelling cot.

It boasted a filthy uncovered foam mattress that was torn in places. A round window allowed daylight to penetrate the dingy hold. It also illuminated a ladder leading to a hatch above.

She tested her legs by applying a little pressure. They were weak and shaky but she just might make it. Joey stood and worked her way toward the ladder, holding onto the cot and then the wall for balance.

She was reaching for the ladder when she heard footsteps on the deck above. They drew closer and her mind scrambled for a plan of attack. There was nothing in here that she could throw or use as a blunt weapon, and she certainly wasn't strong enough to fight as she had been trained. Cagey. She needed to play it smart.

Joey quickly retraced her steps and sank onto the mattress even as the hatch opened and a pair of legs clad in dark coloured cargo trousers descended. She laid completely still, her eyes closed, remembering the effect the drugs had had upon her and trying to replicate it.

Boots landed with a thump onto the floor and then clomped over to the bedside.

"Still out 'ey?" a familiar deep, voice rasped. "Should be close to wearing off by now."

A strong hand gripped her arm and shook her roughly. She wanted to scream, to claw at his face, to run. Yet knowing her life and her freedom depended upon her ability to pull this off, she remained limp and uttered not a sound. She could feel his fingers bruising her tender skin.

He took her hand, pulled her upright and then tossed her limp body over his shoulder. "You'll do."

Where was he taking her? Joey kept her ears attuned to her surroundings as he climbed the ladder and walked her through the boat onto what she guessed was the deck. She could hear the engine idling.

So we're stationary. What is he up to?

He dumped her haphazardly on a flat wooden surface. The fall hurt but she continued to play dead.

"Come on." He nudged her with a boot. "I know you can hear me. The shot I gave you should have worn off by now. I wanna know why the navy is on Pearl Island."

Should she give up the sham? No, not yet.

His tone became ominously dispassionate. "It doesn't really matter. They'll never find your body."

Footsteps retreated and she opened her eyes, chancing a peek to see what he was doing. He was in the wheelhouse not three metres away. Joey's eyes widened in horror as she watched him insert a needle into a small bottle and withdraw the liquid inside. Was he going to give her another dose and toss her overboard?

She frantically glanced around for something to hit him with and spotted a gaff, which was usually used for pulling very large fish from the water. She got to her knees and grabbed the implement.

Her captor noticed movement from the corner of his eye and turned to face her. A sadistic smile toyed with lips that were partially hidden by a dark, thick beard.

"Playing games with me, Jessica?"

She stood on wobbly legs, gaff in hand ready to defend herself. He took three slow menacing steps toward her, needle clasped threateningly in his fingers.

"This can be quick and painless or slow and agonising. Which would you prefer?"

By the look in his dark eyes, she knew he was serious. A small tattoo of a skull upon his cheek twitched with a malevolent glower and she knew she was about to die. She was too physically weak to win this battle.

"God, help me?" The desperate plea came out in a terrified whisper.

"Ain't no God gonna help you out here."

He lunged.

The needle came down and was thrust into her back as he grabbed her in a fierce bear hug. She cried out at the sharp stinging sensation and pulled the gaff down hard. It's sharp hook cut into his left upper arm and he growled with pain and shoved her aside.

The needlepoint broke off and the syringe clattered to the deck half-empty. Joey hit the edge of the boat with her right shoulder and rolled onto the floor.

"Why you..." He cursed and removed the steel hook, inspecting the wound for several seconds.

Feeling the drugs quickly taking hold, Joey struggled to her knees, holding the edge of the boat. She forced herself to stand on weakening legs, her eyes scanning the deck for something else to keep him at bay.

The needle.

She picked it up and blinked several times to maintain focus.

His gaze snapped from the gash in his arm to her face and then the syringe. He lunged at her with an angry growl, grasping the hand that held it. She was too weak to fight back. He angled what was left of the point down and was about to thrust it into her, when he caught sight of something behind the vessel.

Joey didn't know what it was, but his eyes widened in alarm. She followed his line of vision and saw sleek grey steel forging determinedly through the ocean toward them.

"The navy!" He spat the words and returned his furious gaze to the small woman beginning to sag.

She had not received a full dose, but what had entered her bloodstream would be enough to render her powerless to the waves. The navy ship was bearing down upon them. She could almost see the thoughts chasing across his hardened features.

He banged her hand against the side of the boat. The syringe slipped from her grip into the churning water behind the vessel.

He glanced at the ship approaching and looked horrified to see a RHIB full of armed men speed past the ship's prow. It would only take them another minute to catch up. Hope entered Joey's soul.

His boat wasn't fast enough to outrun a navy inflatable. As quickly as hope had flared, it was snuffed out when he spun and thrust her overboard.

Cold water hit her with merciless force. The shock was enough to awaken her dulled senses momentarily. She struggled to stay afloat.

The drugs were taking full effect and she was losing almost all muscle control. Her arms refused to paddle and her legs would not kick. She took a desperate last breath and her head slipped beneath the surface. Her lungs screamed for oxygen but were denied.

Although filled with panic and aware that she was sinking, Joey's mind was once again hazy. Everything seemed almost unreal.

Sinking. Sinking. Blue fog all around her.

Her body relaxed with the drugs and her oxygen-starved lungs drew a breath and inhaled salty seawater. She coughed and inhaled more, choking, drowning. The blue haze around her melded into oblivion as she passed out.

~

Coz leaned over the edge of the RHIB and shouted. "Bubbles! See those bubbles!"

Farmer, who was at the wheel, eased back on the power and before an order could be issued, Lon dropped his weapon and dove overboard.

Lieutenant Donnelly, who had been next to him, knelt on the floor of the boat and leaned on the rim. Should he go in too?

Beside him Wilko and Coz waited, holding their breath in suspension. Ollie and Woody clambered over the seats to get a better view of the water where the bosun had gone in.

Bubbles continued to float to the surface. Something yellow and red was coming up quickly.

A second later Lon surfaced gasping for breath. He had inflated his bright yellow life jacket which had propelled him up. His right arm firmly encircled a woman in a red cotton dress. Joey.

Lieutenant Donnelly and Wilko leaned far enough over to grab her arms and pull her in. There wasn't a lot of space in the RHIB and her lifeless body ended up in the XO's arms, her legs half over the edge.

Coz paled. "Is she alive?"

"Farmer!" Wilko called, even as the ship's medic pushed past the other men and knelt at the unconscious woman's side.

He felt for a pulse. "Quick, put her on her back on the

floor."

The lieutenant disentangled himself and laid Joey flat while Wilko and Coz moved to allow them space.

Farmer placed his left hand atop his right upon the centre of her chest and began CPR. "You do the breathing and I'll take compressions."

Joshua tilted her head back with his left hand, swept wet dark hair from her face and positioned his right hand on her chin. After thirty compressions he placed his mouth over hers and exhaled. Her chest rose and then fell.

They continued the pattern and checked for a pulse after one minute had passed. Still nothing. They began again.

Woody and Ollie pulled Lon from the water while Wilko informed the captain of the situation using the hearing piece and microphone looped around his ear, and the transmitter button clipped to his boarding jacket. The radio itself was tucked securely in a pocket in his vest near his left shoulder blade.

Coz ran a distressed hand through his hair as he watched the nightmare unfold, guilt written all over his countenance.

Lieutenant Donnelly was lowering his mouth for another breath when he heard a gurgling sound and Joey's eyes opened. He quickly rolled her onto her side in time for her to cough up a belly full of seawater.

The boys let out a cheer and Coz sighed with relief. Lieutenant Donnelly and Farmer exchanged relieved grins.

"Sir, they've managed to revive her," Wilko transmitted with a beaming smile.

Joshua leaned over to look into her face. "Joey, talk to me."

Her eyes were glazed and she remained motionless. He glanced at Farmer in alarm. "Something's wrong."

The petty officer felt her pulse and listened to her breathing again. Judging by his puzzled reaction, both must have been steady. So what was going on? Had the lack of oxygen caused brain damage? Farmer checked pupil dilation.

"Hang on, that's not right. Her eyes aren't responding like they should. It's like she's drugged."

The lieutenant remembered the details she had shared with him the night before. He grabbed her arm to inspect it. There was bruising, but it was not accompanied by a needle mark. However that did not mean she hadn't been injected somewhere else.

"Joey." Farmer held her face between his hands and looked into her glazed eyes. "If you can hear me blink twice."

Her eyelids slowly closed and opened two times.

"Were you given anything? Blink twice for yes and once for no."

Her drowsy eyelids blinked twice.

"Ollie, take us back to the Hartfield," the lieutenant ordered. They would need to contact a doctor back in Cairns.

"What about the guy who did this?" Wilko pointed to the vessel speeding into the distance. "He's getting away."

"He won't get far. We can trace his course by radar." Joshua rose and took hold of one of the metal bars in front of the seats as Ollie turned the RHIB.

Coz dropped to the floor beside Farmer and pulled Joey's limp body into his arms. The men around him seemed to understand. They found handholds as the RHIB picked up speed and skimmed over swells on its way back to the ship.

14

"Where are we going again?"

Rylie stumbled and fell a moment later. He landed on his hands and knees and shook his head in frustration. He was almost back to full strength, but his eyes were still a little slow to focus.

He sat and squinted in the direction he had come and finally saw the offending protruding root. He rubbed his eyes and focused on the tall figure striding toward him through the jungle.

Charlie squatted beside him and stared into his exhausted face with a concerned expression. "How are you feeling? You don't look so good."

"I'll be alright. Are you sure we're not lost?" He gazed about at various distortions of green. If he moved his eyes slowly, he could focus. If he quickly scanned his surroundings, it was all one big blur. He closed his lids tightly and opened them again.

"We're going southeast, cutting across the island to the other side. I figure we'll come across fresh water soon. There's bound to be an inland stream somewhere."

Charlie stood and surveyed the area. Rylie was dying of thirst and his stomach was rumbling. He had been drugged for well over a day without food or water. He wondered if his problem wasn't so much the drugs wearing off, but dehydration and weakness from lack of nourishment.

"Hang in there, mate. It shouldn't be much longer."

He struggled to his feet. "I'm fine."

"Sure." She smiled in amusement as he wavered slightly from side to side.

He smiled sheepishly. "Okay, I'll admit I could do with a huge burger or a bucket of KFC chicken. What about you? If you could eat anything right now, what would it be?"

Charlie grinned and wove her way through the jungle. "An enormous chicken wrap and a pile of doughnuts for dessert."

"I'd have the biggest drink of coke I could get my hands on."

"Nah, a huge milkshake sounds more like it."

They exchanged grins.

"Maybe the pirates will have food. We could swipe some when we help Dad escape."

Rylie shook his head but did not argue. Her crazy idea of hunting down the pirates and stealing their radio was as close to insanity as he figured a body could get. His best bet was to find a safe place to hide until help arrived, but not Charlie. He was quickly discovering that she was a woman of action. It was comforting and scary at the same time.

~

Commander Kelly's solemn gaze passed over the officers gathered for a brief meeting in the ship's office. His eyes rested upon their coxswain. "How's Joey doing?"

"She's conscious and vaguely aware of things around her, although she's still unresponsive. I've taken some blood samples for pathology to analyse."

They stood in a rough circle, the XO, Wilko, Lon and Farmer. Shep was at his navigation station on the bridge, as was Jaffa who was still monitoring communications.

Commander Kelly's expression was grim. "I've been in touch with Admiral Broderick who has been liaising with the federal police. They think they've found a connection between Rylie Hunter's kidnapping and Joey's. It turns out she's been taken before, four years ago in fact. Back then her name was Jessica Hyndman."

It was news to everyone except Joshua, and several brows rose in surprise.

"Her father owns a shipping company called Pacific Nova. Rylie's father is Ezekiel Hunter, owner of Hunter Shipping Lines, as you know. The feds have been investigating company documentation since the hijacking of The Kelly-Ann and have extended their investigation to Pacific Nova Shipping as well. It seems both companies have inconsistencies in their records."

Lieutenant Donnelly tried to decipher the connection. "So it's likely drugs were smuggled through Pacific Nova as well?"

The commander nodded gravely. "Yes. The owners of both companies are being investigated. Our concern now is recovering the boy and the hostages. We've been informed that Hunter Shipping Lines is unable to come up with the money for ransom. They're negotiating with the hijackers but it's not looking good. If we can get to them first without jeopardising the hostages, it would be the optimal solution."

Lon frowned. "So drug smuggling through these two companies is the connection between Rylie and Joey's kidnappings?"

"Yes, it would seem so. Although no one can understand

why they were taken and no ransom was demanded," the commander answered. "The supposition at this point is that it was some kind of threat to maintain cooperation with the smuggling. Any more questions?"

"Yes sir," Lon spoke up. "Are we taking Joey to the hospital on Pearl Island?"

The commander shook his head. "No. The doctor back in Cairns has been conferring with Farmer and wants to examine her properly, but we can't afford to abandon the chase now. She's stable and apparently whatever she was injected with is wearing off. She hasn't suffered any ill after-effects from the sea water in her lungs. It sounds terrible and I wish it wasn't this way, but she'll have to wait. That boy is still out there and it's likely we'll find him if we follow Joey's kidnapper."

Lon appeared highly dissatisfied. "You're right, it does sound terrible."

Joshua shot him a warning glance.

Lon was quick to clarify his remark. "Although I understand the logic."

"Our plan is to follow that boat. It looks as though it's heading for Gabriel Island, which is only an hour away. We'll have two RHIBs with seven on board each ready to do a reconnaissance of the island should he get that far. Lieutenant Donnelly, I'll leave that up to your discretion."

"Yes sir."

"Are there any more questions?" The captain met each man's gaze enquiringly. When no one spoke, he nodded with his usual decisiveness. "Dismissed."

~

"I've told you this before," Ezekiel answered Jack, who was sitting in his hotel room at the resort. "I wasn't the one that handled cargo manifests. You'll have to speak with my executive, Ian Rochester. He's been basically running the company on his own for the past year." He was standing at the window overlooking the bay.

The coast had taken a battering the night before but thankfully the worst of the storm had passed them by. Today the sky was bright and clear without a sign of a cloud anywhere.

Federal Officer, Jack Coleman, was sitting on the sofa taking notes. He paused and glanced up curiously. Ezekiel's thick, short hair was dark, with a small smattering of grey around the temples. Jack guessed they were roughly about the same age. There the differences ended.

Where Ezekiel was of average height and sturdy build, Jack was over six foot and lanky. Ezekiel's features were finely sculpted and would be considered attractive by the opposite sex. Jack had a hawkish nose and a dimple in each cheek that had over time weathered to become crevices.

"Why has your executive been running the company for the past year?"

Ezekiel glanced at him through troubled eyes. "My wife was diagnosed with a cancerous tumour and had to undergo surgery and ongoing treatment for months afterward. I stayed home to care for her and for our son." His sad gaze returned to the scene out the window. "This was our first trip away together since Elizabeth received a clean bill of health."

Jack studied him quietly. So many things were beginning to make sense. It was no wonder Ezekiel did not have the money for a ransom. His family had probably been living on their savings in order to keep the company afloat.

"Tell me about your executive, Rochester isn't it? How long has he been working for you?"

The businessman turned to study Jack with a perplexed frown. "You don't think he had something to do with the drug smuggling, do you?"

Jack smiled reassuringly. "I'm just trying to cover all of the bases."

Ezekiel nodded. "He has been working for me for roughly two years. He came highly recommended from his previous executive roll at Pacific Nova Shipping."

Jack's brows winged upward. "Do you know how long he worked at Pacific Nova?"

"You would have to ask him." Ezekiel's gaze was straight-forward and unguarded.

The federal officer's mind was working double time. "I most certainly will."

~

"'... Death is swallowed up in victory. O Death, where is your sting? O Hades, where is your victory? The sting of death is sin, and the strength of sin is the law. But thanks be to God, who gives us the victory through our Lord Jesus Christ. Therefore, my beloved brethren, be steadfast, immovable, always abounding in the work of the Lord, knowing that your labour is not in vain in the Lord.'"

Coz stopped reading from Joey's Bible and glanced up at her with a curious frown. He opened his mouth to comment on the passage and the words died on his lips. Her eyes were closed and her breathing was shallow but steady.

They were in the wardroom and she was lying on the table that had been temporarily converted into a bed. Switch and Katie had been delegated the task of removing her wet clothes and dressing her in a grey navy issue t-shirt and camouflage trousers from her room. Her long black hair was almost dry. Along with her clothes, Katie had kindly brought the cook's worn Bible.

"She likes to read this every day. It means a lot to her." She had avoided Coz's eyes and hastily exited.

It had been most upsetting to listen to Joey's uneven breathing and witness the silent tears that slid down her cheeks as Farmer withdrew blood, which was to be tested when they reached port in Cairns. The medic had then been required to attend an officer's meeting and had left her in Coz's care.

The horror of Joey's ordeal hit him when he finally under-stood the awareness she had of everything around her and her powerlessness to respond. He had taken Katie's advice, opened Joey's Bible, and begun to read. He was only a para-graph into Corinthians thirteen when her breathing calmed and the tears stopped. He had kept reading and now in chap-ter fifteen she had finally fallen into a peaceful sleep.

He glanced at the verses he had just read. What did they mean? The idea of death being swallowed up in victory and rendered powerless sounded wonderful. His family were Catholics and he had attended mass since childhood, but he had never really paid much attention to what was being said, and he had never read the Bible. What did the law have to do with sin? And how did Jesus Christ give victory over it all?

He heard footsteps in the passageway outside and closed

the book. Several pages were coming loose and were protruding and he had noticed that Joey had underlined certain
verses and written in the margins. Prior to reading to her
only moments ago, he never would have understood her fas-
cination with it. Now, a strange yearning welled within him
to know and understand for himself.

Lon poked his head in the doorway. "How's she doing?"

Coz glanced at the bosun and then returned his gaze to his
friend. "She's sleeping."

The enormous mountain of a man stepped into the room,
making it seem so much smaller. Farmer followed.

Lon came to stand beside her. "Are you sure? It's kind of
hard to tell since she can't move or talk."

Farmer gently felt for a pulse in her wrist. Strong and
steady. "No, Lon, you'd have known if she was awake." He
looked to Coz in some amazement. "How did you get her to
calm down?"

The young man held up Joey's worn Bible. "I just opened
this and started to read. Her breathing evened out and
her eyes became peaceful. Then she just drifted off." He
shrugged, a gesture that belied the stirring in his heart to
experience that peace for himself.

Lon's expression was sceptical. "The Bible! Don't ask me
how that could possibly help."

"I didn't know she was religious. Although I did wonder
why she was different from the others."

Coz and Lon looked at Farmer in surprise.

"Don't get me wrong," he hastened to explain, "everyone
on board is great, but you've got to admit that Joey is different."

Lon rubbed the back of his neck, his expression suddenly

thoughtful. "Yeah. Most of the boys swear like troopers and they can be a bit coarse at times. I've never heard a cuss word out of Joey yet. She's always even-tempered and ready to make you laugh."

Farmer chuckled. "Is that why you tease her more than the others?"

He shrugged. "I guess. She's a good sport."

"Good woman that." Wilko nodded toward the sleeping patient. He was quietly standing in the doorway, and had obviously overheard their conversation.

Lon, Coz and Farmer stared at the chief engineer in surprise. The simple comment was high praise coming from the macho, emotionally uncommunicative sailor.

A hard glint entered his indignant eyes. "Reckon I wanna wrap my hands around the neck of the bloke that did this to 'er."

"You're not the only one," Lon remarked.

Coz secretly agreed with them, although something told him Joey would not be pleased with their vengeful attitudes.

15

Masculine voices floated through the passageway accompanied by scuttling feet. Joey stirred and opened her eyes. The room was a white blur. Where was she? She squinted and her eyes slowly came into focus.

She was in the wardroom aboard the Hartfield. She closed her lids in relief and a single tear escaped down her cheek. She raised a sluggish hand to wipe the insubordinate droplet away.

I can move!

She sighed deeply and rolled onto her back. She briefly scanned the room. Coz and Farmer were gone, and if the shouts and scuffling on the deck above could be trusted, something was going on.

How had they rescued her? Her mind returned to the small fishing vessel and her kidnapper. She remembered struggling with him and being tossed overboard. She even remembered sinking, but from there things were a little hazy.

Someone had held her on board some kind of vessel and must have carried her onto the Hartfield. She remembered another needle going into the tender flesh of her elbow and the horror and frustration it brought with it. Then a voice had drifted into her semi-consciousness with words so familiar and comforting that God's peace had surrounded her.

Now everyone was gone and she was lying in the wardroom. Should she try to get up? Joey raised her head off the pillow and then her shoulders. The effort caused her to pant with exertion and she lay back down. Her whole body felt weighted with lead. She recognised the sensation and old memories arose to haunt her afresh. How could it have happened again? Why hadn't God protected her?

She rolled her head left and something small, square and black snared her attention. It was lying next to her, partially hidden beneath her pillow. She shifted onto her side again and clasped her Bible in both hands. A surge of anger tore through her. She was tempted to toss it across the room, convinced God had failed her.

I preserved your life, did I not? The foreign impression confronted her anger head on.

Joey mentally cringed. As much as she wanted to scream that life was unfair, to rail at the world and even at her Maker, she withheld the torrent of emotions tumbling inside her like a storm tossed sea. This was God she was dealing with, and although He was understanding and compassionate, He was still the infinitely powerful Creator of the universe.

I want to trust You but I have no trust left. I want to believe You love me and will protect me, but You didn't.

Open and read, He gently prompted her battered heart.

Part of her resisted, and then remembering the comfort His words had brought her so many times over the last three years, she opened her Bible to a random passage and squinted to focus.

'Who can find a virtuous woman, for her price is far above rubies.'

She stopped, unable to go past verse ten in Proverbs thirty-one. What did 'virtuous' mean? She glanced at the cross reference in the centre column. Valour. She frowned. A woman of valour?

Lord, I don't understand. What does this mean?

She waited in silence, hearing voices call above her and machinery at work. It sounded like one of the RHIBs was being lowered. Another minute ticked by and she reread the verse, unable to move past it. She puzzled for another three minutes and finally thoughts that were definitely not her own dropped into her mind.

A virtuous woman is valiant, honourable, strong and courageous.

Joey's eyes widened in surprise. Words continued to fly directly to her heart as swiftly as arrows to their target.

A strong woman endures, bears up under the pressure, does not budge from the way of righteousness. She is brave in rising to the task, in dealing with strong willed people, in facing hardship and suffering. She is honourable in that her conduct is above reproach, her behaviour above question. She is rare among the daughters on earth. So rare that her price is above the most precious stones.

Joey's heart stirred with desire and challenge.

"I want to be like her. I don't want to be afraid anymore."

Bravery isn't the absence of fear, daughter. It is rising to the task regardless. It is facing hardship and suffering even when you know it will be difficult, even when you know it is going to hurt you and cost you; even when you would rather turn and flee for your life. Be assured, I am with you every step you must take through the valley of the shadow of death.

She sensed the strong and comforting presence behind those words and the tension inside her snapped loose like shackles falling from the hands of a prisoner. Her tears came in earnest then.

She wept for the loss of her family, her innocence and her trust. She cried broken and angry sobs for the violation of her will and her freedom. As the past played before her mind's eye, words rose within her and she began to speak them aloud.

"'...Death is swallowed up in victory. O Death, where is your sting? O Hades, where is your victory? The sting of death is sin, and the strength of sin is the law. But thanks be to God, who gives us the victory through our Lord Jesus Christ. Therefore, my beloved brethren, be steadfast, immovable, always abounding in the work of the Lord, knowing that your labour is not in vain in the Lord.'"

She quoted it over and over again until it sank deep into her spirit. Finally the tears that flowed brought healing. She quoted those verses one more time and drew courage from their depths, courage she would need to face the very near future.

~

Farmer drove the RHIB's nose onto the beach next to the inflatable raft already on the sand and cut the engine. The seven sailors aboard leapt over the edge and dropped to the sand, semi automatic weapons in hand.

"Alright," Lieutenant Donnelly addressed the crew, "his boat was empty and this is his dingy, so he's on the island somewhere. He may be armed so be careful. Ollie, you stay with the RHIB. Wilko, you come with me. We'll head inland to the northeast following these footprints. Lon and Farmer, head to the northwest in case he turned off in that direction once he reached the trees. Woody and Switch, go southeast. Stay under cover of the jungle and radio in if you find anything. Okay, we'll rendezvous back here in an hour."

Without another word Joshua nodded to Wilko and they headed into the jungle directly before them. Each team struck out on their search in the designated direction, poised for action and eyes alert.

Joshua wove between debris and fallen trees with Wilko close behind. The storm must have hit the coast of Gabriel Island with a vengeance. The jungle was eerily silent and the sound of waves lapping at the shore faded into the distance. They walked on stealthy feet, eyes scanning the battered forest around them.

"Hey," Wilko whispered sharply, "what's that?" He pointed to an incline not ten metres away. A large tree had crashed through what appeared to be a small hut.

Joshua smiled shrewdly at the chief engineer. "That, Wilko, appears to be what we're looking for."

Wilko grinned in return. Joshua signalled with his hand for his partner to come in from the jungle on their left, and he circled right. He crept steadily toward the hut, carefully stepping over fallen branches. He reached the damaged structure first.

The huge tree had fallen across the ramshackle dwelling diagonally. Beneath the buckled tin and fractured boards, he could see what appeared to be a bed. There was no possible way anyone inside could have survived the impact of the tree.

However, the man they were hunting could not have been inside when it fell. They had been tracking his vessel through the storm by radar. If this hut truly belonged to Joey's kid-napper, there was a distinct possibility that the boy might be inside. He had come back to this part of the island for a reason. To kill the boy and remove the evidence? Joshua was not certain. Either way, they had to get a better look inside.

He looped his rifle over his shoulder, and with one glance at Wilko to ensure he was keeping watch, he began pulling tin roofing and broken boards away from the wreckage. The tree partially covered a rusty, wrought iron bed, yet he was able to see ropes tied to the bed head.

He reached around the thick trunk and pushed branches aside to get a better view. He fingered the closest rope which had been severed.

"Wilko, someone was tied to this and then they were cut free."

"The boy or The Kelly-Ann hostages?"

"I suppose it could be either. Hang on."

Joshua saw a glint of light bouncing off an object on the dirt floor nearby. He reached through leafy foliage and debris and picked it up. He had no idea how it was possible that the small bottle had not shattered when the tree hit, but some-how it had survived the impact.

He removed the cap and sniffed, pulling a disgusted face at the pungent aroma. What was this stuff? He could make a pretty good guess. He fished around on the floor some more, pushing aside leaves and twiggy branches.

Finally his fingers landed upon something smooth and cylindrical. He lifted it from its dark hiding place beneath the tree and what appeared to be a smashed crate and studied it in the light. A syringe. He held it up for Wilko to see, a know-ing eyebrow raised.

A moment later something hurtled through the air, seemingly from nowhere, and collided with the engineer's face. Joshua leapt from the wreckage, items still in hand and crouched beside his fallen comrade.

A thin trail of blood trickled down the left side of his partner's face from a cut on his cheek. Beside him was a fist-sized rock. Joshua shook him and gained no response. He dropped the bottle and syringe beside his mate and swung his weapon off his shoulder into his hands. His wary eyes studied the thick jungle around them. With his left he pressed the transmission button clipped to his bullet-proof vest and spoke through the radio headpiece looped around his ear.

"This is x-ray requesting backup immediately. We're directly northeast of the RHIB, roughly one-hundred metres into the jungle. Wilko is down and the attacker is nearby. Do you copy?"

"Roger that x-ray. This is-"

A solid body crashed into Joshua from behind, tackling him to the ground. His face hit the dirt and his weapon was wrested from his hands. He rolled onto his back, grabbing the semi automatic rifle gripped by his attacker still upon him.

Their gazes locked as they struggled for possession of the gun. Hateful eyes that glinted amber in the light stared into Joshua's, and a small tattoo of a skull on the villain's cheek above an unkempt beard burned itself into his memory.

His attacker brought his elbow down hard into the side of his face. Momentarily stunned from the blow, he loosened his grip. The villain stood and aimed. Joshua stared into the barrel and panic hit him like a punch to his stomach. He swung his left leg into the back of his opponent's knees, toppling him to the ground. The weapon discharged into the forest as he fell.

Joshua lunged for it with his left while swinging with his right. His solid fist connected with his assailant's jaw and the struggle ceased.

He ripped the rifle away from the unconscious man and stepped back, barrel aimed at the broad chest which was clad in a dark t-shirt with a skull blazing in a fire. The man's stereotypical image reminded him of a biker.

Joshua's breathing came hard as adrenaline charged through him. He quickly scanned his surroundings in case this man was not alone. Footsteps crashed through the jungle toward him, coming from the direction of the beach. He spun in time to see Ollie burst into the small clearing, weapon in hand.

"Don't shoot!" he shouted in alarm as the lieutenant's rifle swung in his direction.

Joshua sighed in relief and lowered it. "Sorry Ollie. I thought for a moment that this guy might have company."

Ollie's wide eyes landed upon the large man sprawled near the XO's feet and then drifted to Wilko lying several metres from them. He groaned and stirred.

"And to think when we pulled out of port in Cairns I thought this was going to be a normal patrol!" He strode to the chief engineer's side to offer assistance.

16

Rylie dropped to his knees beside the river rippling peacefully through the jungle and drank deeply. Beside him Charlie did the same. When his thirst had abated, he splashed his face and neck and sat back on one of the large boulders lining the stream. His vision was clear and his mind was sharp, and both were working overtime.

He examined the wild terrain around them. The intense tropical sun beat steadily down through the canopy of thick jungle foliage, yet the tall trees on all sides seemed to keep the atmosphere to a bearable balmy temperature.

The stream was deep and crystal clear and flowed merrily through the wilderness, oblivious to the undercurrent of evil washing through the island at that very moment. But Rylie sensed it.

The hair on the back of his neck stood on end and his spirit was ill at ease. Charlie was determined to find the pirates and get her father back and it worried him. He sensed a reckless pride in her which scared him more than the threat of finding the brigands that had taken her. An overestimation of self could lead to mistakes and ultimately capture and death.

She stood and her gaze drifted through the forest and across the river. "It shouldn't be too far now."

Rylie looped his arms casually over his knees while he studied her. "What makes you think that?"

She withdrew her compass from her pocket. "I can hear the ocean again, which means we're probably close to the other side of the island."

"Why do you think they'll be on the other side? This place is big. They could be anywhere." He much preferred his plan to wait in a safe place for help to arrive.

Charlie's brows knit in concentrated study as she glanced at her compass and then mentally calculated their position. "I figure all we need to do is go to the next high point and take a look around. I scouted the south shore and saw nothing. From the next peak we'll be able to see the north shore. That would be the likely place for them to hide because it was sheltered from the storm. They're nasty but they're not stupid."

Rylie sighed and stood. "And how exactly are you planning on getting into their camp without being seen?"

Charlie shrugged and waded through the river to the other side. "I'll figure that part out when we get there."

He shook his head. "Sounds foolhardy if you ask me." He began praying for a solution, knowing that he needed to keep a cool head on his shoulders.

~

Joey heard the commotion above deck and sat up. Her vision was back to normal, and although she was still a little weak, she had full movement of her body.

Coz had looked in on her regularly, but he seemed distracted. He had explained that Lieutenant Donnelly had taken a shore party to look for her kidnapper. She had spent the time in prayer, also thinking over the Lord's counsel regarding the proverbs thirty-one woman.

She felt ashamed for initially wanting to throw away her relationship with God when things had become difficult. She realised that now was when her faith would prove genuine, or just a sham. She could let this tear her apart or allow God to strengthen her through it and somehow use it for good. She decided on the latter.

Footsteps sounded in the passageway outside the wardroom. Commander Kelly's stocky frame filled the doorway and he smiled to see her sitting up. His green eyes softened with kindness.

"You're looking much better. You were asleep when I saw you last."

"Yes sir." An uneasy feeling came over her. "You've found him, haven't you?"

"Yes, Joey, we have," he answered in a gentle tone.

She sensed a hesitation in him and understood why. "You want me to identify him."

"Yes. And we need to hear your account of what actually happened."

You're right, Lord. I want to run. This won't be easy.

'Be steadfast, immovable, always abounding in the work of the Lord, knowing that your labour is not in vain in the Lord.'

She drew a deep breath. *Okay God, here we go.* "Let's get it done then."

She slid from the table to the floor with a look of steely determination. At first her legs threatened to buckle, so she grasped the table and leant against it until she was steady.

"Are you sure you can handle this? I can come back later."

"I'm fine." Joey fortified her heart. "Let's go."

Rylie bent to retie his shoelace. Charlie pushed ahead, shoving large leaves aside with her hands where dangling vines and undergrowth were dense. A strange feeling came over him and urgency pressed upon his sensitive heart. He glanced up at the girl ahead of him, sensing that it was her at risk.

"Please, God, protect her?"

A moment later she fell hard. A split second afterward a massive vine-covered beam swung from in front of her horizontally like an arm. It passed over her and crashed with a thud into the tree to her right. Rylie's heart leapt into his throat and he sprang to his feet and ran toward her.

Charlie sat up and looked first at Rylie dropping to her side and then at the massive beam that had barely missed her. "What was that?"

"Are you okay?" Adrenaline charged through his veins. "You nearly got plastered to a tree!"

She frowned in bewilderment and stood. "What happened?"

The two studied the horizontal beam that was now embedded in the tree. Rylie circled the contraption. It was a medium sized straight trunk that had somehow been suspended and spring loaded. On the side that would have struck Charlie were long protruding nails positioned closely together.

"It's a booby-trap. Something must have triggered it." His eyes scanned the forest floor near where Charlie was standing and then he spotted it. Strung tautly across the rough-hewn trail was a thin wire. "You must have set it off by tripping on that."

He pointed to the trigger and Charlie's stunned gaze dropped to the wire she had landed on.

"I've heard of traps like this. They used them in Vietnam during the war." He circled the tree again to stand beside her.

She looked at him through wide, fearful eyes. In her expression, he saw that she finally understood she had almost died.

"Just as well you pushed me down when you did!"

Rylie frowned in puzzlement. "I didn't push you. I was back there tying my shoelace."

Her astonished gaze held his. "But I felt a hand push me down. That's why I fell."

His brows rose in surprise. "Wow." He remembered the urgency he had felt and the prayer he had whispered. "That explains it then."

"That explains what?" She stared at him in confusion. "Did you see someone push me?"

"No, and I was watching you the whole time. There was no one there." He suddenly grinned. "It was an angel. It had to be."

Charlie snorted in disbelief and a smile tugged at her lips. "Good one. You actually had me going for a moment."

"I wasn't kidding. I didn't touch you and I didn't see anyone. Just before you fell I had a strange feeling that something was wrong and that you were in danger, so I asked God to protect you. The next second you were on the ground and that beam whooshed over the top of you."

The sincerity in his eyes wiped the smile from her face. "Rylie, this isn't funny. There is no such thing as angels and there certainly isn't a God anywhere out there. Drop the gag and tell me the truth. I felt your hand between my shoulders and you pushed me really hard."

Rylie could not help the grin that parted his lips and revealed straight pearly white teeth. "I promise you on my life that I did not touch you, and that's saying something because I don't make promises."

"Rylie, you're scaring me!" She spun angrily on her heel. With her eyes sweeping the forest floor, Charlie gingerly continued in the direction they had been heading.

He started after her. "Then explain it to me. I saw the whole thing. Nobody was there! It had to be God!"

"You're just trying to scare me." She glared at him over her shoulder.

"Whatever you reckon," he muttered and directed a smile heavenward. *Thanks God. You and I know differently.*

~

Joey stared at the picture of the man cuffed to a bunk in the auxiliary accommodation berth. Although generally it was used for transporting soldiers or detainees, today it had another purpose. Aside from the twenty bunks either mounted to the walls or bolted to the ceiling and floor, there was no other furniture, making the sparse room the perfect place to hold their prisoner.

She was on the bridge in front of a computer screen. Jaffa had downloaded the photo he had taken of the prisoner from his digital camera and as Joey stared at it her blood ran cold.

Numbness stole over her. "That's him."

Commander Kelly studied her with unnerving perception. "Is he the man that kidnapped you the first time as well?"

She swallowed hard, took a deep breath and nodded.

Lieutenant Donnelly was also watching her reaction carefully. "You're sure?"

She was aware she must look awful.

"You were out of it with drugs for the most part," he reasoned logically.

"It was like the first time. I knew what was going on around me. And I'll never forget that face!"

Commander Kelly nodded calmly. "Okay. Can you tell us what happened?"

Joey's face drained entirely of colour and she began to tremble all over. She was grateful for the seat beneath her. Without it her legs would have buckled and she would undoubtedly be on the floor. The other four occupants of the bridge, the captain, the XO, Shep and Jaffa, faded from view as her mind replayed her ordeal in vivid detail. She was vaguely aware of her voice retelling what had happened, however the images took centre stage. She finished with her struggle with her captor aboard the commercial fishing vessel. "From there you all know what happened."

Jaffa, who had recorded the statement using a microphone on the desktop that fed into the computer, turned the device off.

"Thank you, Joey," Commander Kelly said gently. "Will you be alright to head to your berth? I want you to rest up until we reach port."

She nodded absently, not really comprehending what he was saying. Her vision was still full of haunting memories. She numbly wandered from the bridge, and instead of going to her room, quietly made her way to the quarter deck.

~

Everything inside Joshua demanded that he follow her and ensure she was alright. The officer in him required he stay at his post and do his job.

"Sir, I'd like Farmer to check in on her regularly today. She's still in shock."

"I can see that." Commander Kelly's concerned gaze lingered on the stairway where the usually feisty ship's cook had descended from view. "Jaffa, will you call Farmer to the bridge please?"

"Yes sir."

"And then get a hold of the federal police. They'll be very interested in this turn of events."

17

Joey sank to the deck with her back to the waist-high steel railing. She was still trembling from head to foot and images from the distant and recent past played out before her eyes. Instead of blocking the barrage, she stared into them, allowing the pain and confusion to surface.

Okay, Jesus, I'm facing it. Walk with me through this valley?

She felt His presence surround her. As she faced the darkness she had hidden deep inside, she sensed a light of hope pierce its heavy gloom.

She did not know for how long she sat like that, praying and remembering, but finally Joey lifted her eyes and saw the sky above the Hartfield aflame with sunset.

She rose stiffly to her feet and stood at the railing. She realised as she watched the sun splash its golden reflection upon the rippling ocean, that the heavy pall that had clouded her soul had lifted.

She was free. Free from fear, free from the pain and grief she had carried for so long, free to love, free to forgive, free to live.

A gentle smile touched her lips and her heart sang a joyful song, like a bird on the very first spring morning after a long dark winter. Joey lifted her hands to the sky in silent praise to the Liberator of her soul.

"Thank You," she finally whispered, and lowered her hands to her sides.

~

Lon, who had been about to refuel the RHIBs, paused as he came around the corner of the deck and witnessed the scene. He felt like an intruder into a very private moment. He was tempted to leave as quietly as he had come, but knew that refuelling the RHIBs was not something that he could put off.

He opted instead to retrace his steps, clomping his boots loudly on the deck as he rounded the corner a second time.

Joey turned at the rail to see who was approaching and an easygoing smile tugged at her lips. "Hi sailor. It's been a big day."

Something in her expression had him baffled, and at the same time it drew him toward her. The RHIBs slipped from his mind as he looked into her peaceful eyes. He rested his elbows on the railing beside her, yet was unable to take his gaze from her face. How was such serenity possible after all she had been through?

She looked at him questioningly. "What is it, Lon?"

He lowered his macho defences in a rare show of honesty. "You're so... so peaceful. I can't understand it."

A serene smile appeared. "That's because I've had a long talk with Jesus. He's in control."

Lon glanced unseeingly out over the ocean. "See, that's what I can't understand. How can you still love Him when He let you go through that? You were kidnapped and drugged and the guy that did it tossed you overboard to drown. You died today, Joey! Your heart actually stopped beating and it took two men to revive you! There may be a God, but He certainly doesn't care about you or me. How can you keep loving Him?"

Lon's blue eyes, which were usually wreathed in lines of laughter, were filled with confusion and pain.

Joey's eyes misted over the hurt he had experienced. "Oh Lon, I'm sorry you had to go through that." Compassion filled her gaze. "But there's something you need to know."

His jaw clenched and he fought back tears.

"God warned me not to leave the ship, but I ignored it. Had I listened to that impression I felt, I would have dropped the matter of my purse and simply checked in with the watchman and gone to bed. But I didn't. I think the fact I'm standing here alive before you is proof that God does care."

"But Joey, He could have prevented it altogether. He could have stopped that man." Lon pointed toward the island off their port side where they had apprehended the kidnapper.

"He did. The twisted maniac is below deck in cuffs. And besides all of that, there's something you need to understand about God."

The bosun glanced toward the sunset, yet missed its magnificent beauty.

"It's people who choose to do evil, not God. He won't stop us from choosing to do wrong, because in doing so He would also be stopping us from choosing to do right. Choice is a gift and He leaves it up to us what we will do with it.

"That man chose to do evil, which affected me and has affected the boy he's probably taken too." She gestured to the deck where in the bowels of the ship Zacutti was cuffed to a bunk. "But the beauty of choice, Lon, is that I don't have to be chained by what he did. I can choose to forgive and even to love. Now that's what God intended when He gave us free will." Joey stared into his rather resistant face.

Lon's eyes flamed with anger. "That guy doesn't deserve forgiveness! He deserves hell and the sooner the better."

"And so do I," she replied calmly. "As does every human being on the face of the planet."

Her reply shocked him speechless and he stared at her aghast. She then had the audacity to smile in amusement, and a gleam entered her warm brown eyes.

"How about I explain that one."

"Yeah, I think you'd better."

Joey leaned on the railing and let her gaze wander over the vast waters stretching before them. "Touched by crimson... The ocean like this always reminds me of another day that ran with scarlet."

Lon puzzled silently over her cryptic remark.

"The problem with this world is that everyone lives by their own set of standards. God has standards that He governs the universe by and expects us to live up to. Only, He is the authority behind them and has the right to execute judgement on those who break His set of laws.

"The Bible says that every person on the face of this planet has broken them at one time or another in their lives. It says that all people are sinful, whether from stealing, killing, lying, or even a hateful or lustful thought. He will hold us accountable for every deed, every word and every thought, and He can do it because He is perfect and has never sinned. I'm just so grateful that He really does love us and is merciful. And by merciful I mean that He made a way for us to escape judgment, and hell that would surely follow.

"It began the day a perfect baby was born, Jesus Christ, the Son of God, God in the flesh. Even more incredible than God coming into the world as a human being was the purpose for which He came, to die on a Roman cross bearing the punishment, which was death, for all mankind. Like I said, a day that ran with scarlet.

"Equally mind blowing was that He came alive three days later. Now anyone who believes in Him, asks His forgiveness for all they've done, and lives in a close relationship with Him, is guaranteed eternity in heaven when they die and His matchless companionship and help while they live.

"That's why I have peace, Lon. I know where I'm headed when I die and I don't have to be afraid. And just as important, I know Who to go to when I need healing, comfort and help."

Joey looked him directly in the eye as she finished her explanation and her gaze softened. "The question is, do you?"

Lon stared at her in amazement. He had heard about Jesus, but never put like that. Never someone he could know personally. And eternity was another matter. He had never known full assurance was possible. It was something he wanted.

"I'll admit it. I want what you've got, Joey. I just don't know how."

She smiled softly and her eyes sparkled with joy. "Pray with me."

Lon had a sense that this moment was likely the most important of his life. He swallowed hard against the lump rising in his throat and nodded. They closed their eyes, and there with the sun splashing its last scarlet rays upon the day, they began to pray.

~

Darkness was falling, but it was not the darkness of night time that worried Rylie. It was the evil that shrouded the island like a moonless night.

Since their encounter with the booby trap, they had come across two more trip wires, one designed to trigger another spring-loaded beam, the other a grenade without a pin. Thankfully they had noticed them both and simply stepped over.

A place to stay the night was now their concern. The last ray of light faded from the sky just as they came across a hole in a hillside close to the north shore, covered by green leafy foliage.

With their hearts pounding in their ears, the two explorers squeezed inside and found a small, empty rock cavern. At some point in time it had probably been a den for an animal, now it housed two hungry, frightened teenagers.

Charlie readjusted the leaves across the entrance so that it was not obvious and they settled in for the night, neither one having any inkling as to what the following day might bring.

~

"The crew of the HMAS Hartfield have found the man we believe is responsible for your son's kidnapping," Federal Officer Jack Coleman informed the boy's parents that evening.

They were sitting around a small mahogany table in their large suite at the Southern Star Resort. Ezekiel and Elizabeth exchanged hopeful glances.

"And Rylie?"

Jack's grave gaze held theirs and he spoke the words no parent wanted to hear. "They found the place they think he was holding the boy, but he was gone." Seeing the fear and distress in their faces, he hurried on. "Now, that doesn't mean he disposed of the boy, it could mean that Rylie escaped. It would seem Zacutti, that's his name by the way, headed into Abbotsford cove on Lila Island to hide from the storm. There he kidnapped and drugged one of the crew of the HMAS Hartfield who had recognised him.

"He set sail again for Gabriel Island. The Hartfield tracked him down by radar and rescued their crewmember. They then caught up with Zacutti on Gabriel Island where they found a small shack damaged by the storm. We believe Zacutti returned to do away with the boy, although he denies he took him. However, with his history of abduction and other details that are coming to light, it would seem that he is our primary suspect."

Ezekiel clearly distasted the words on the tip of his tongue, but went on to voice them. "What makes you think he hasn't killed our son?"

"An enormous tree crashed through the shack onto the bed inside. The navy found evidence that someone had been held against their will there, but they said it would have been impossible to remove them from beneath the tree.

"We know for certain that Zacutti was not on the island during the storm, and by the time he returned the shack was already in ruins. Ropes tied to the bed head had been cut, suggesting that someone has removed the hostage before the storm."

A puzzled frown furrowed Elizabeth's brow. "He could have taken him before the storm, or he might have had a partner."

"When Zacutti's vessel was found, we were able to track down its previous owner who had sold it only a few days before. The previous owner identified a picture of Zacutti and assured us he was alone. Also, that same vessel was seen exiting Crystal Bay on Pearl Island the evening of your son's abduction. The local fisherman that saw it leave the bay also said he watched a man go on board carrying something large across his shoulder. It was very dark and he couldn't be sure of what it was, so he put it down to provisions. We believe it was Rylie."

Jack did not want to give false hope, however the facts suggested that it was possible the boy had escaped. He just hoped that the villain hadn't dropped the boy in the ocean as he had the cook aboard the Hartfield, or they would never find the body.

Ezekiel appeared both hopeful and frustrated at the same time. "So what are you saying? That someone else has our son? Or that he's somewhere on Gabriel Island?"

"Yes. Someone cut those ropes at the shack and the sooner we can investigate the island, the sooner will find out what happened there. I'm sailing to Gabriel in the morning. I just thought you would like to know what we've found so far."

Ezekiel and Elizabeth held one another's gaze. Ezekiel answered for them both. "Yes, thank you."

Jack nodded and rose from his chair. He strode toward the door and turned with his hand on the knob. "We will find him."

Ezekiel nodded. Elizabeth thanked the officer one more

time before he quietly left.

~

Husband and wife stared at one another. Ezekiel read hope and excitement in Elizabeth's lovely eyes. He did not want to snuff it out, but within him the dark voice of doubt whispered that he might never see his son again this side of heaven.

18

It was late the same night when Joey padded softly into the galley. She and Lon had missed dinner, but neither had cared at the time. Then Farmer had finally found her and escorted her to the sick bay for another check up. She had found her bunk and rested for a while before hunger finally drove her to the galley in search of food.

She flipped the light above the stove on and opened the refrigerator. Inside she found some leftover lasagne from dinner. She rubbed her hands together and eagerly reached for the dish.

Joey sat it on the bench beside the fridge and foraged for a spoon and a plate. Within minutes she was sitting down on the floor of the galley with her plate laden. With a prayer of genuine thanks, she dug in.

She was just finishing her last mouthful when a tall figure stepped through the galley doorway. She came to her feet quickly and took a step backward.

"It's just me," Coz's subdued voice reached her ears. "What are you doing up so late? I thought you'd be out like a light by now, all things considered."

From the tone of his voice, the day's events had to be weighing heavily on his mind.

Joey gave her plate and spoon a wash in the sink and put them away before turning to study him. "What are you doing up?"

Turmoil had darkened his eyes. He leaned against the counter beside her. "Couldn't sleep."

Something in Joey's mind triggered a memory, like a light switch flicking on and illuminating a room.

"In the RHIB today, someone was holding me. That same person also brought me on board the Hartfield. Coz, it was you, wasn't it?"

She held his troubled gaze and suddenly his face crumpled and emotions he had obviously kept at bay all day crashed over him like a breaker on the shore.

Joey's heart ached for him and she hugged him around the waist. His arms came around her shoulders and he held on tightly. She could feel salty droplets landing on the top of her head.

She fought back tears of her own. "I'm so sorry you had to go through that, Cozzi."

"When they pulled you in, you weren't breathing and I knew it was all my fault," he confessed in a deep, soft voice.

Joey stepped back to look into his face in bewilderment. "What are you talking about? You had nothing to do with me being kidnapped."

He wiped his cheeks with a sleeve and avoided eye contact. "If I hadn't been such an idiot, you would have simply spent the evening with me playing pool and you never would have been on the dock when you were."

"Don't be stupid, Coz. None of you are to blame. Not you, not Jaffa, not Woody and not Lieutenant Donnelly. Zacutti is to blame, no one else. So you just drop that line of thinking, you hear me?"

He smiled at her sisterly tone and sniffed. "Now you sound

like your old self, telling me what to do."

Joey clouted his arm with her open hand. "You watch yourself, young pup. Respect your elders, or at least respect that I outrank you."

His smile broadened and then it faded as he stared at her pensively. She returned his gaze questioningly.

"What is it?"

"What does that stuff you read mean?"

"What stuff, Coz?"

His face was open. The bravado and pretence he usually wore in front of the men was completely gone. "In your Bible. That stuff about death being swallowed up in victory. What's it about and how does Jesus Christ fit in?"

Joey marvelled at yet another opportunity presented her in the same day to share about her Jesus. Interestingly enough, it was all as a result of what she had suffered. She was beginning to feel that it had been worth it just for this.

"May I tell you my story?"

He shrugged. "Sure, but will you get to the part about Jesus and death getting swallowed by victory?"

She smiled warmly. "Most definitely. Pull up a chair," she invited with sparkling eyes, aware that there were no chairs in the galley. Joey sat on the floor and leaned against the cupboards.

Coz smiled in amusement and sat down beside her.

"It began four years ago when I was kidnapped the first time by Zacutti. I've never told you this, but my father was worried the kidnapping was an attempt to get at him. He drove me interstate, changed my name, gave me money and took me to enlist in the navy. He told me not to contact them until the kidnapper was found. As you know, that didn't happen until today."

"So you still haven't heard from him?"

"No. I'm hoping now it will be possible. Anyway, I was in the navy about a year when I met the chaplain assigned to my division. The crew was on furlough for a week and I had nowhere to go. I offered to do more hours on the base and we met there.

"We talked for a while and got along really well. He had a bunch of friends coming over that night for a barbecue and he invited me along. I met his wife and children and his guests. They were all wonderful.

"We had a marvellous time and when he invited me along to the church where they all went, I accepted. I was lonely and I had no one but my shipmates, and they were all on holiday with their families and friends. I knew nothing about church or God and was absolutely fascinated during my first time there.

"I didn't understand all of what was said, but I felt God's presence and I felt the love of His people. They took me in like one of their own and suddenly I had a family. It was through them I came to understand about Jesus, and when I did, I asked Him into my life.

"You see, Coz, the sting of death is sin, and the strength of sin is the law, that is our standard and it holds us to account. The sin in our lives has a cost and the cost is that we are separated from God forever, and when we die we will go to hell. But thanks be to God, who gives us the victory through our Lord Jesus Christ!

"When Jesus, God's only Son, died two-thousand years ago, He paid the cost for us and took our punishment. When He rose again from the dead, He made it possible for everyone who believes and accepts Him to do the same. Not necessarily to rise from the dead physically, but spiritually.

"He promises that those who ask His forgiveness for their wrongdoing and ask Him into their lives will one day stand in His presence in heaven when their life on this earth is over. That is why death and hell have lost their sting and their victory. They have no power over the person in relationship with Jesus.

"Zacutti could have taken my life today, and I would have closed my eyes here and opened them in the presence of God Himself in heaven."

Joey's penetrating gaze met and held his. "Coz, are you ready to face God as you are, or do you need to do what I did three years ago and ask His forgiveness for the things that are separating you from Him?"

Coz shook his head in denial. "I'm a good person, Joey. I've never stolen anything or killed anyone. I've saved myself for marriage and I've done a lot of good deeds. I don't see that I need His forgiveness. And for that matter, I don't see how you do either."

Joey chuckled softly.

A bewildered frown puckered his brow. "What?"

"Cozzi, have you ever burned a copyrighted CD or told a lie?"

He looked at her sceptically and shrugged. "Sure, but that's not really so bad. It's not like I've ever hurt anybody."

She raised a knowing eyebrow. "Have you ever back chatted your mother or father?"

Coz sighed and reluctantly admitted, "Yeah, I guess."

Joey bit her lower lip and grimaced. "I hate to be the one to tell you this, but according to God's law you're guilty."

He shuffled so that he was fully facing her. "You can't be serious. How do you figure that?"

Joey could not resist a smile of amusement, which he returned. "God's commands require that you shall not steal, you shall not lie and the clincher, honour your mother and your father, and that's just three out of ten. Do you want to try the others?"

All amusement fled and his expression grew serious. "It does say that, doesn't it? I'd forgotten."

"Coz, you're just as guilty as I am, but what worries me is that you haven't taken care of this with God. I have and although I'm not perfect, He is slowly changing me and helping me to do better. When I fail, I ask for His forgiveness again. I do my best to keep my account with him short. Is your account in order, or if you stood face to face with Him right now would you have to pay the cost?" She quietly watched his reaction.

"Wow, you've got me." The comment was unruffled, but behind it, he appeared slightly shaken. "This ain't good."

Joey sought his gaze. "Coz, I'm not trying to make you feel bad and I'm certainly not saying I'm any better. I'm also not trying to pressure you into anything. But you did ask me."

He blew out his cheeks. "Yeah, I guess I did. Can I think about it?"

She smiled warmly. "Sure. But with pirates in the area and the chance we might get shot at, I wouldn't be thinking too long."

He chuckled. Once on his feet, he stretched. "Good point. I'm going to bed. Will you be alright?"

Joey outstretched her hand and he pulled her to her feet. "I'm more alright than I've ever been. I'm more worried about you."

He smiled easily and ruffled her hair before turning and wandering from the galley. She watched him go and a smile played about her lips.

"Wow Lord," she murmured, when he was gone, "You're incredible! Twice in one day! I can't wait to see what tomorrow holds."

With a prayer for Coz and for her shipmates, Joey strolled back to her room and quietly crawled into her bunk. Something told her she would need all the rest she could get.

19

"They're onto us."

Ian Rochester was using his mobile phone while navigating late night traffic, as he desperately sought an avenue of escape from his situation. He planned to throw as much into his suitcase as he could in three minutes and hightail it to the nearest airport.

He had already shifted his final laundered payment to the offshore account under a false name. He would tell his wife it was a business trip, and by the time the authorities caught on to what was happening, the money would be gone and so would he.

"What makes you think that?" the chillingly cool voice replied over the mobile connection.

Ian made a sharp left onto his street. "They've been going through company records and asking me detailed questions about cargo manifests. They've discovered the inconsistencies in the company's accounting."

A sinister chuckle rumbled on the other end of the line. "No, my friend. They're onto you, not us. You knew the risks when you joined my venture. You're on your own."

Ian felt livid at the ruthless devil he was dealing with. "You took my boss's daughter and demanded I cooperate! What kind of a choice was that? I never wanted to be a part of it. You can guarantee that if I go down I'll pull you under with me."

"And just how will you do that? You've never seen my face and you don't even know who I am or where I live. All you know is that I follow through on my promises, and I promise you that the day you help the police, is the day I'll have you eliminated."

Burning with rage, Ian hit the end button on his cell phone and pulled into his driveway. Yet again he was stuck between a rock and a hard place. "Not if I can get out of the country in the next hour."

He climbed from his vehicle and strode up the pathway to the front door of his luxurious two-storey home. Just as he was reaching for the handle, the door opened and a familiar masculine face stared back at him from the entrance.

"Welcome home, Mr. Rochester."

Ian quickly recovered and smiled with surprise at the federal policeman. "Officer Lawton. I thought we concluded our discussion at my office an hour ago."

Dylan Lawton stepped aside to allow him inside. Ian placed his briefcase by the door and turned to the man before him in the foyer.

"What can I do for you at this late hour?"

A petite, cuddly blond in her early fifties stepped into the foyer from the living room. Her grey eyes watched her husband with a gravity he had never seen before. She knew.

"I'm afraid I haven't come to talk, Mr. Rochester. You're under arrest for drug smuggling through Pacific Nova Shipping Lines and Hunter Shipping. Anything you say can and will be used against you in a court of law..." The officer continued to recite his rights while another stepped from the living room and came up behind him with handcuffs.

Ian listened to the monologue with a strange mixture of astonishment and rage. It was all his fault, whoever the mastermind really was. Whether Ian would die as a result or not, he determined right then and there to make good on his threat and help the feds catch the villain in any way he possibly could.

~

Rylie pushed through dense foliage, noting that the thunder of rushing water was growing louder. Charlie followed him, her alert gaze missing nothing in their surroundings.

They had encountered two more booby-traps in the last ten minutes since they had left the cave. One had been a large pit with spikes protruding from the bottom, which Rylie had narrowly escaped falling into when his foot slipped through netting covered with leafy debris.

The second had been a snare that Charlie's shoe set off. A fishing net had sprung from beneath the leaf covered forest floor where she had been standing, and had drawn her up into the treetops by a series of ropes and weighted pullies like a sack of squealing monkeys. Once again her multi-tool came in handy and she cut her way out while Rylie rolled around on the ground laughing.

Thankfully the short walk had not been entirely unfruitful. They had discovered a small valley abounding with wild fruit not five minutes from the cave they had slept in.

Yet now as they approached what sounded like a waterfall, they were wary. This jungle was a death trap. Rylie moved a large leaf aside with his right hand and stepped forward at the same time. His heart leapt in fright when his heel connected with solid earth but his toes met only thin air. He teetered and took a step backward.

Once he had regained his balance and his courage, he leaned forward enough to push aside the last couple of large tropical leaves blocking his view. His eyes widened in awe.

He heard Charlie's soft exclamation from behind him as she looked over his shoulder.

"Wow!"

Below was a fifteen metre drop into a river roiling from the falls cascading down another sheer cliff face to their right. Directly across from them the forest continued on even ground, as though someone had taken a large shovel and scooped out the gorge in a long rectangular shape between each section of jungle.

"Maybe we could swing across on one of those vines." Charlie pointed to one of the vines dangling nearby like a thick piece of rope from a treetop high above them.

Rylie glanced at her sceptically. "That only ever works in movies."

Charlie shrugged, more than willing to give it a try if it was their only alternative.

He passed her a dry look. "Let's follow the river and cross above the falls."

She gave him a sheepish grin, clearly not having considered the logical alternative. "Okay, you win."

They struck off to their right through the jungle.

"But my way would have been more fun."

He glanced over his shoulder with an amused gleam lurking in his sea green eyes. "Before or after we plummeted to our deaths?"

Charlie laughed and followed with eager footsteps. Her

sense of adventure seemed to be irrepressible.

~

"The federal police have arrived to investigate the crime scene," the captain informed the crew that were gathered on the quarter deck and standing at attention. "Meanwhile it's our duty to scout the island. We'll be looking for the boy, but be careful. It's also possible we might come across pirates.

"The hijacking of The Kelly-Ann happened not many kilometres off this island. Of the five islands in the Pearl Isle, Lila is the closest to the hijacking. Gabriel is next. It's much larger, and as you know uninhabited. It would be the perfect place for a hideout as it's so inhospitable and difficult to traverse.

"I'll be dispatching both RHIBs, seven crewmembers in each. One crewmember will stay with each RHIB while the others travel in groups of three. You will be fully armed and I expect you to be on the alert. Maintain radio contact at regular intervals and cover as much ground as possible.

"You will be covering ground on a grid so that you don't go over the same areas twice. Those not ashore will remain to man the ship and provide assistance to the federal police. Are there any questions?"

Joey had one, but she kept it to herself. She wanted to search for the boy and yet the captain had stood her down from duty because of his concerns for her health and wellbeing. True, she was still sore from Zacutti's attack, but she also knew that she was well enough to undergo the mission.

When no questions were forthcoming, the captain handed over to the executive officer to announce who would be going ashore. Joey knew great disappointment when her name was not read, although she understood why. She was, however, delighted for Coz who had been included in the lengthy list.

She sighed and went below deck. Seven crewmembers were left aboard including the navigator, the radio operator, the captain, the electronics technician, a sailor from engineering and a deckhand. That meant there was no cook.

Well, we'll soon see about that.

Joey determined to rectify the situation. She'd go mad if they would not let her help out in some way, even if that meant stepping back into the galley. She sought out Farmer and then Lon, hoping they would be able to persuade the captain to allow her to take up her regular duties.

~

"Lon, have you ever considered the possibility that God's standard of right and wrong might be higher than ours?" Coz asked thoughtfully as he followed the bosun through the jungle on the south side of the island.

They had been methodically covering their area on the map for well over an hour and had found nothing except splintered branches and fallen trees. Behind them, Woody's vigilant gaze scanned the damaged forest, then directed a curious glance at his shipmate.

"Not until yesterday, mate," Lon replied honestly as he too studied the surrounding terrain they were carefully picking their way through. Only days ago it had been lush jungle.

Coz was surprised by this answer. "What happened yesterday that made you think of it?" He stepped over a fallen branch.

Lon's eyes roved meticulously back and forth. "A rather re-markable little woman shared her faith and I decided it was what I needed too."

Coz's brows shot upward in surprise. "You believe in Jesus like Joey does?"

The enormous bosun turned with a grin for his shipmate. "Yep. I'm a brand new Christian as of last night."

Woody's expression quirked in astonishment. "I didn't think you were into religion."

"I'm not. But I'm sure into Jesus. You should've heard the way Joey explained it." He returned his gaze to the terrain ahead as he talked. "God coming to earth in the form of a baby. Growing up and dying to take the punishment for the times we've broken God's standards, and then coming alive again. Just amazing! I think her exact words were '...anyone who believes in Him, asks His forgiveness for all they've done, and lives in a close relationship with Him is guaranteed eternity in heaven when they die, and His matchless com-panionship and help while they live.'

"That's why Joey's got peace, you know. She knows where she's headed for eternity, and Who to go to when she needs help. Now I do too." Lon cast him a serious glance. "You ought to think about it, Coz. You too Woody. None of us live forever."

Coz felt a familiar inner stirring. If a big tough bloke like Lon had accepted Jesus, then perhaps this Christianity thing wasn't just for the weak and wretched. However, if Coz was honest with himself, he did feel wretched and weak inside.

Joey's challenge the night before had hit home. If she was right about God's commands, and from his upbringing he knew she was, then he truly was guilty and condemned to pay for breaking them. No amount of Hail Mary's or absolutions from a priest could acquit him. That reality was sobering and more than a little frightening. What was he to do?

You know the answer to that question.

Maybe he was just being paranoid because of the possible danger they were facing. He could live to be an eighty year old man and set things right with God later when he needed to. On the other hand, life held no guarantees. The tragic death of his best mate in high school proved that.

In fact, it had been that very event that set his course for the navy. He had determined to make better choices with his life than his friend who drank heavily, and subsequently one night after a party crashed his car into a tree.

There were times, however, when Coz's desire to fit in overrode his determination to leave that life behind, such as New Year's Eve. He regretted that. Joey had been right. His mother would have been ashamed, but not more than he was.

I am sinful, he finally admitted to himself. Jesus, I need You. Forgive me? Change me from the inside out to be a better man, the man you know I want to be?

With that simple prayer came a sensation that he had never known before. He felt clean, as though the filthy rags of his errors had been stripped away and replaced by a fresh garment. Something else accompanied it, gentle and restful. He smiled when he realised it was peace.

20

"Charlie wait."

She was walking ahead of Rylie at a slow, careful pace. Around them the jungle was roomy. Huge ancient gnarled trees reached for the sky, sprouting leaves high up in the canopy. Interwoven amongst their twisted trunks and branches were thick vines with large waxy leaves.

The forest floor was littered with short undergrowth and a layer of dried leaves, bark and rotting wood. Humidity hung heavily in the air, causing perspiration to dampen the teenagers' clothing.

Charlie stopped and turned to him. "What is it?" She was slowly learning to listen when he sensed something was amiss, and by the foreboding look on his face, he was experiencing that right now. Although she found it disconcerting, she was beginning to acknowledge he had a knack for knowing when bad things were about to happen.

He attributed it to his sensitivity to God. She did not agree, however she was unable to deny that his uncanny intuition had been correct every time.

"I don't know. Something isn't right." Rylie wiped beads of sweat from his brow with a dirt-smudged shirtsleeve. His wide wary eyes roamed the forest around them for danger. "Please God, if someone bad is out there, make us invisible to them?"

Charlie raised sceptical brows and rolled her eyes. She shook her head and continued up a small rise. Rylie hung back, his feet rooted to the spot.

At the top of the small hill Charlie's foot stepped on what looked like solid ground and heard an ominous metallic click. The leafy earth gave way to a rockslide. She lost her balance and tumbled down the short slope along with a host of fist-sized rocks rolling all around her.

Finally the rough ride stopped and she lay at the bottom of a small flat gully cleared entirely of shrubbery, but now littered with rocks. She winced with pain and lay still to gauge the damage. Her right ankle felt sprained. Her arms, wrists and hands were smarting, as was her back and knees.

Although nothing felt broken, she could feel bruises forming and knew she must be covered with cuts and abrasions. She lifted her head from the ground and looked back up the slope. Her eyes widened in astonishment.

A large fishing net that previously had been covered in leaves disguising the rocks, now hung limp from a three-metre drop off into the gully, along with two outstretched steel rods with hooks on the ends.

Peeking from beneath the strewn rocks, where she now tried to sit up, was a barrier wall that had been held upright by the rods. It had fallen over when she stepped on what she now knew must have been a metal plate attached to the rods, triggering the hooks to release their hold on the wall. The rocks that had been contained had subsequently tumbled free. Another cleverly thought out booby trap. She could have kicked herself for falling right into it! Rylie had been correct again.

He appeared at the top of the drop off anxiously looking

for her. He spotted her at the same time a trap door dis-
guised by moss and leaves in the forest floor, swung up and
open in the centre of the small gully not five metres from
where she was sitting.

They both froze and watched in stunned paralysis as a
head with medium length jet-black hair and then two arms
appeared, one with a tattoo of a venomous snake on it. In
the islander's hands, one of which bore a picture of huge
spider on the back, was a semi automatic weapon.

Charlie recognised him instantly and horror filled her. He
stepped into the clearing from his underground hideout and
with weapon brandished, suspiciously studied his surroundings. Wherever his eyes went, the rifle barrel followed. His
gaze swept right over her as though she was not there.

Rylie dropped to his stomach, but the pirate did not seem
to even notice the sharp movement which was in plain view.
His gaze swept the clearing one more time and landed upon
the top of the drop off.

Something rustled in the shrubbery beside Rylie. A wild
boar trotted from the bushes, snuffling the earth for grubs.

"It was just a wild pig that set it off!" the pirate shouted
down the hole in the ground.

Charlie watched in astonishment as he aimed and fired.
The animal, only one or two paces away from her friend,
dropped to the earth dead. Rylie covered his head with his
arms as bullets whizzed past his ears. The shooting stopped
and the pirate laughed.

"I shot us a feast!"

His comrades poured out of the trap door fully armed like
a colony of bull ants from its nest.

Charlie recognised each one of the men from the zodiac.

Scarface, Bandanna, Blue Eyes and the stocky one with eyes as black as his soul. She stared in astonishment and utter bewilderment as three remained close by while the other two charged up the slope to their right to fetch the downed animal.

Why couldn't they see her? And for that matter, why hadn't they spotted Rylie?

"We'll take it further inland to strip it of meat and cook it," Scar-face called down to Bandana who was waiting by the trapdoor. "That way no one will see the smoke."

"Alright, just make sure you bring it back for the rest of us, or you will end up like the pig." There was a glint of humour in the leader's otherwise callous eyes.

Something told Charlie that even though he seemed to be joking, he would carry out the threat should Scar-face fail to comply.

Scar-face grinned and he and Snake-arm carted the dead animal into the jungle. The three pirates in the gully descended back into their lair and the trap door closed with a thud.

Rylie glanced up from the dirt where he had remained with his arms flung over his head. The sound of footsteps retreated into the jungle, and in the distance waves lapped at the shore. Not even trying to understand what had happened, he got to his feet and scrambled down to Charlie who was still sitting amidst a pile of rocks in a state of shock. He helped her to her feet and she winced with severe discomfort, favouring her left foot. He placed one arm around her waist and she automatically dropped an arm around his neck. He clasped it with his free hand and helped her limp out of the gully into the jungle.

She panted from exertion and glanced at him question-ingly as they topped the rise. "What happened back there?"

Rylie shook his head in amazement and kept going. "My guess? It was God again. Are you still clinging to your atheist worldview?" He grinned at her sideways.

"I'm beginning to have serious doubts," she admitted as they hightailed it out of there.

~

Joey passed a meal to the last sailor that evening. The teams sent to Gabriel Island had spent a fruitless day search-ing and were experiencing a great amount of discourage-ment. Finding any signs of human life on the island seemed next to impossible, let alone a boy.

The federal police confirmed Lieutenant Donnelly's suspi-cion that the boy had been held captive in the shack. DNA tests taken aboard Zacutti's pleasure craft, the shack and samples previously gathered at the Hunter's hotel suite were a perfect match. Zacutti had taken Rylie.

As for what had become of the boy prior to the kidnap-per's return to the island, that was a mystery. Forensics were still working on finding a match for the extra fingerprints they had found at the scene.

They were beginning to think that he had been killed before the storm and his body disposed of, although the evidence for that theory did not add up. All the same, the navy crew still had at least sixty percent of the island left to search. Tomorrow would be a long, tense day.

"How are you holding up, Joey?" Lieutenant Donnelly asked, the recipient of the last meal.

"Fine thanks." She had been asked that question repeatedly throughout the day, the captain having checked on her several times himself.

After seeing the proficiency with which she performed her job and her calm manner, he had eventually shelved his concerns for the time being and left her to her work.

Joshua's volume lowered and his concerned gaze held hers. "Are you sure?"

Joey smiled to reassure him. "I really am alright. I would even like to help with the search tomorrow."

He studied her silently. "I don't think that's such a good idea. You need rest and time to process things right now, and if you were to come along and we found something, it might trigger a reaction. I'm not willing to risk that. Not to mention it could jeopardize the mission."

"I've dealt with what happened, and although I can't promise it won't come back to haunt me on occasion, I seriously doubt it will." Joey looked him squarely in the eye, her own gaze pleading for understanding. "I need to help find that boy. I think helping would provide more healing than hanging around the galley all day. I'm a doer, sir, not someone who likes to sit on the sidelines."

Joshua's gaze was compassionate. "Be that as it may, Joey, I need you here."

Joey's brows knit in confusion. What did he mean by that? That she was needed aboard ship? Or that he needed to know she was safe? She doubted it was the latter, because the XO was professional to the core.

Yet as she studied him, she saw a vulnerable light enter his kind blue eyes. Could it be that he cared about her on a more personal level?

"You know I'll do as I am ordered, sir." She shoved the crazy notion aside. "But should another sailor be needed on the island, please remember that I volunteered? If you're worried about my health or something like that, check with Farmer. He says I'm fine."

The Lieutenant's expression grew stern. "He's not a doctor."

Joey wanted to argue. Farmer was an experienced medic who knew what he was doing. Sure he was not a qualified doctor, but he was the next best thing.

The lieutenant must have read the resistance in her expression, for a gleam of guilt entered his eyes.

She dropped her disappointed gaze. "Yes sir." She turned from the counter to the plate she had kept aside for the prisoner. The lieutenant took his meal to the wardroom, the matter obviously closed in his mind.

Lord, I know it won't be easy, but I want to do this. I feel physically able and I want to help. If it's okay with You, will you please change the XO and the captain's minds? Leaving the matter in God's hands, she faced her next challenge. Zacutti.

"Who is that for?" Coz watched her remove her apron and lift a spare meal in her hand. Her dinner was on a plate beside his keeping warm.

She answered with a quick glance his way. "It's for the prisoner."

He immediately dropped what he was doing and reached for the plate. "I'll take it."

She moved it behind her. "Thanks for the offer, Coz, but this is something I have to do."

His uncertain gaze held hers. "Are you sure?"

154

She sighed in exasperation. "I wish everyone would quit worrying about me and just except my answers for what they are!"

His brows hiked upward. "Phew, take it easy Joey!"

She drew a deep breath to control her frustration. "I'm sorry for snapping. Thank you for caring, Cozzi, but I really am alright."

A smile tugged at his mischievous lips. "And to think I was worried about *you*. I aughta be more concerned for the bloke you're taking that to."

Joey hid a smile. "That's more like it Seaman Corrado." She stepped around him and heard a chuckle as she exited the galley.

Not many minutes later she was standing outside the prisoner's quarters. Wilko was taking his turn guarding the door. He glanced at the dinner in her hand and then at her face in surprise.

"I didn't think they'd send you to deliver his food. Someone else should be handling that."

"Coz tried. I wanted to do it myself. Open up will you Wilko?"

The chief engineer hesitated for a moment and then reluctantly unlocked and opened the auxiliary accommodation door. He stepped in ahead of her, fully armed.

"Your food's here, although if it were up to me I'd let you starve."

Zacutti, who had been lying on the bunk against the far wall, sat up. His malevolent eyes locked onto the small cook as she entered the room. A tremor of fear ran through her and she wanted to run.

Who can find a virtuous woman... The phrase drifted

through her mind. Virtuous. Valiant, courageous, strong.

Help me be like that?

There was no immediate reassurance or voice from heaven, but as she took her first step toward the man who had caused her so much fear and grief, another verse popped into her thoughts. It gave her the grace and courage to cross the room.

'...be steadfast, immovable, always abounding in the work of the Lord...'

Joey kindly handed him the plate. "Here is your dinner."

He took it with the hand not cuffed to the bunk. His surprised gaze went from the delicious food now in his possession to the woman before him. She remained in place holding eye contact and radiating peace, which apparently made him hate her all the more.

"What do you want?"

"I have something I need to say to you." Joey swallowed her fear and her chin jutted out stubbornly.

"Get lost! I wish you'd drowned." He disregarded the knife and fork on the edge of his plate and used his fingers to pick up a piece of chicken. He took a bite.

"That's just tough luck, isn't it." She drew a deep breath and then spoke the words that would grant her complete release. "I forgive you."

The prisoner's bitter eyes swung upward to meet hers. "I don't want your forgiveness!"

A mischievous little smile played about Joey's lips as freedom spiralled through her. "Well you've got it whether you want it or not." With that she turned and calmly walked out.

She felt Zacutti's livid eyes bore into her back, but she did not care. She was free. She smiled at Wilko as he closed the door and resumed his post, and noticed his look of absolute astonishment. She passed him a wink and strode back to the galley.

21

"We've traced the origin of the opium you helped to smuggle, Mr. Rochester," Federal Officer Dylan Lawton stated calmly.

He was sitting in the interview room at the station downtown, the only furnishings being a table and three chairs. Upon the left wall was the exit and set into the adjacent wall, a large window. It was a mirror. On the other side of it, federal officers were recording the conversation while they watched the interview.

The blank walls were a soft blue to promote calmness, although the accused sitting across from Dylan was anything but calm. His lawyer sat quietly beside him, a sage looking man in a suit who appeared to be in his late fifties.

"Payments were made to Iranian government officials who originally bought the opium from Afghanistan at cost prices. They sold it to the man blackmailing you, at a profit. Sources at Intelligence tell us the money they gained was then used to finance Hezbollah activities and shipping of nuclear weapon parts from North Korea." Dylan's shrewd brown eyes carefully studied Ian Rochester. The businessman appeared to be genuinely horrified and guilt-ridden.

"Why are you telling me all of this?"

"As far as we're concerned, Mr. Rochester, you're a small fish. We're after the man who organised this with the Iranians."

Ian glanced at his lawyer, and then at the officer. "I've already told you that I will cooperate fully."

Ian's earnest expression said he was telling the truth, and alerted Dylan to the fact that this man was no hardened criminal.

"We want you to make contact with him again. As far as he knows, the federal police are onto you but haven't caught you yet. Stay on the line as long as possible and we'll trace the call."

"He's smarter than that. He'll be bouncing the signal off satellites all over the world."

Dylan grinned. "Ah, but we are smarter. You just keep him on the line and we'll handle the rest."

A hopeful light entered his eyes. "You don't suppose this will help me gain a lesser sentence?"

Dylan nodded toward the attorney, who responded calmly in acknowledgement. "Your lawyer has already talked terms with us, and as you know, supported your full cooperation in exchange for a deal." Dylan held the businessman's gaze steadily.

"Mr Rochester, I would advise you to take the deal. Like the man said, you are just a small fish, and it's imperative the man behind all of this is captured. It's not only the smart thing to do, it's the right thing."

Ian absorbed his advocate's advice and finally nodded. The federal officer smiled with glee like the cat about to catch the canary.

"Alright, let's discuss what you will say."

~

Rylie sat down beside Charlie in the small cave where they had spent the previous night. "How's your ankle?"

She looked into his kind green eyes and was struck by what an unusual young man he was. She had only spent three days in his company and her entire perspective on life had been shaken to the core and flipped upside down.

She could no longer deny that there was a God when inexplicable things kept happening whenever Rylie prayed. The supernatural sense he had was also disconcerting. Part of her wished she had never met him so that she could hold onto her rational, very scientific view of the world. Meanwhile the other part was curiously drawn to his dynamic faith. It was real, there was no denying that. What was she to do with it? That was a question she could not answer.

"It's still really sore but I should be able to walk on it."

"I think we'll stay put today. We know where they're hiding now and how to get there. It's time we sit and plan instead of charging in blindly like we've been doing for days. I'll fetch us food and water to last till tomorrow when we go on the hunt again."

For once Charlie did not argue. "Okay."

She felt relieved when he left to find the fruit trees they had been surviving on. She was shaken by the day's events and wanted time to rest and think.

~

The following morning the pirate vessel was located in a secluded cove. It was a relatively new fishing vessel with a zodiac attached by a line at the back. The crew of the Hartfield were allocated task groups to search the north side of the island on a methodical grid.

Daz and Seaman Oldham were placed on guard duty aboard the pirate vessel after it had been searched thoroughly. Ron Debartista, Able Seaman Yusef and Farmer set off to the southeast to comb the jungle. Lieutenant Donnelly, Ollie and Seaman Corey Knight went straight inland. Wilko, Wes and Katie swept to the southwest, while Lon, Graham Steele and Ryan Blackwell headed inland on the grid beside the XO.

Coz and Woody remained with the RHIBs on the beach within sight of the Hartfield and its deck guns should trouble come looking for them. Left aboard the navy patrol boat was the captain, Shep, Jaffa, Switch and Joey.

Four remained behind because they were needed. Shep for navigation, Jaffa for communications, Switch for technical support and the captain to coordinate the mission and maintain contact with command back in port.

Everyone on the island had been provided with packed lunches and those left behind had only to open the refrigerator for the extra sandwiches Joey had made. She was tempted to feel superfluous and yet deep inside she had an awareness that she may be called upon.

With that impression in mind, she dug into the task of preparing a simple meal for the evening that could be placed in the oven to heat up by someone else if for some reason she was not present.

~

"She was totally into me," Seaman Corey Knight stated

with confidence as he regaled Ollie with a tale of one of his evenings clubbing back in Cairns.

"What makes you think that?" Ollie was slightly curious and yet also seemed unimpressed by the young man's infatuation with himself.

Corey grinned and glanced back over his shoulder at his comrade as they traipsed through the jungle. "When we were dancing she-"

"Sh!" Lieutenant Donnelly interrupted from his place several paces ahead of them, his ears picking up a sound incongruent with the forest towering around them.

It sounded almost like a metallic click. From the corner of his eye he saw something hurtling toward him at an alarming rate. "Get down!" He instinctively dropped to the ground.

Corey frowned in confusion and glanced down at his feet when he realised his boot was caught on something. A split second later a sawn log attached to ropes at each end swung down from the trees above, over the top of the lieutenant, and straight into Corey's upper torso. The impact sent him flying backward into Ollie and they landed with a teeth-jarring thud on the jungle floor.

"Are you both okay?" The lieutenant picked himself up off the dirt.

Both Ollie and Corey were down. Corey looked seriously injured. The suspended log had lost momentum with the impact and shuddered in place between the fallen men and the XO. Joshua spotted the trip wire as he quickly closed the gap between them.

"Corey?" Ollie sat up and noted his comrade's struggle to draw breath. "Sir, I think he's hurt bad!"

"He's winded." Joshua dropped to his knees beside the

injured man. "Breath out, not in."

Corey obeyed and exhaled. He then was able to inhale, however that caused great discomfort for he winced with pain and clenched his teeth. "I think my ribs are broken."

Joshua removed the flak jacket and tore open Corey's shirt. His chest was already beginning to bruise and it did appear that several ribs were out of place.

"My right shoulder hurts and so does my arm."

Joshua inspected those next. Corey's collarbone had a telltale indentation and his arm did not look much better. "They're both broken." He pressed the transmission button on the device clipped onto his vest. He spoke into the communication headset looped over his ear. "This is the XO to the Hartfield. We've got a man down. Repeat, we've got a man down."

"Roger that, Lieutenant," Jaffa's voice crackled in his ear. "What's the status of the situation?"

"The island appears to be booby-trapped. Corey set off a trip wire that triggered a large log to swing down from the treetops straight into him. He has a broken collarbone and possibly several broken ribs and a broken arm. Requesting a stretcher and immediate medical attention."

Jaffa's voice returned after several silent minutes where he must have been conferring with the captain. "Roger that. Give us your location. We're rerouting a team and sending you Farmer."

"Much appreciated." Joshua gave them the coordinates. He glanced up at Ollie who had retrieved Corey's rifle and was inspecting it with a look of amazement.

Joshua's brows rose when he saw the buckled weapon. It had clearly taken the brunt of the blow. "Corey, you're lucky to be alive."

The other man managed a shivery smile. Shock was setting in.

"Hang in there, seaman, help is on the way."

~

"We can't spare any more of the crew," Commander Kelly informed Lieutenant Donnelly an hour later aboard ship. "The feds have finished their investigation and are leaving within the hour. They're coming to collect the prisoner and to take Seaman Knight to the hospital on Pearl Island so that we can remain here.

"They said they're sending more men to retrieve the pirates' vessel but until then Able Seaman Altenhof and Seaman Oldham must remain on guard. The Hartfield has a skeleton crew as it is and the only person I can spare is Joey."

"But sir, I don't think that she's up to-"

"Farmer assures me that she is physically able and she seems to be handling things in her usual efficiency. I'm not sending you and Ollie back out there one man down and I have no one else to offer you."

Not liking the situation one bit, Joshua was forced to accept it. "Yes sir."

He could think of several other solutions that would not compromise her health, but he knew he would have to bury his misgivings and bring her along. Would she be able to cope emotionally with danger and tension after her terrible ordeal? He supposed they would all find out.

He knew he wasn't supposed to baby her or treat her any differently than he would the rest of the crew, but if he was honest with himself, he was struggling. He attributed it to having lost Amanda, and Joey's brush with death had brought his grief to the surface again. Or were his feelings toward the feisty chef starting to deepen?

22

"Sir, we've got him." Officer and technician, Lisa Cambridge, had come to the doorway and addressed Dylan Lawton. A triumphant gleam sparkled in her eyes.

Dylan smiled at Ian Rochester who had just finished his conversation with the mystery man. He was sitting across from the federal officer at a desk in a small office just off the large main room at police headquarters.

Through the doorway he could see desks with computers littering the spacious room that was fairly buzzing with activity. However the office they occupied was small with only one workstation and two chairs, one on either side, a computer, a trashcan and a filing cabinet.

Dylan rose from his chair at the desk. "Who is he and where is he?"

Lisa shook her head in amazement. "He was hard to trace but we were able to place him within a one kilometre radius. You'll never believe this. He's in the Pearl Islands, on Blue Jay to be exact."

Dylan's brows quirked in puzzlement. "Out of the five islands, only two are uninhabited. Gabriel and Blue Jay."

Lisa smiled with secret knowledge. "Yes, but Blue Jay was sold six months ago by the government in a very lucrative deal."

Understanding lit Dylan's shrewd brown eyes. "Yes, I'd

forgotten about that. It was in the paper. The Australian ex-foreign minister purchased it, didn't he? Mr. Alexander Pritchard." A cagey smile stretched his mouth. "What do you say we put surveillance on the man and track all of his financial activities?"

~

"We've still got enough daylight to scout around a bit. How's your ankle?"

Rylie was sitting opposite Charlie in the small cavern. They had spent most of the day just sleeping, and now as dusk was coming on, it was time to begin planning.

"Better, although it's still a little sore."

Normally Charlie would have been the one champing at the bit to get out into the action, however yesterday's encounter appeared to have destroyed her confidence.

Rylie knew that if they came across the pirates again, speed would be necessary for escape. "Maybe we should stay put another day."

"No. They've got my father. Somehow we have to help him get away."

Rylie studied her shrewdly. She didn't look as convinced as she sounded. He suspected she was insisting purely out of loyalty. Because if she was anything like him, deep down she had to be scared stiff of leaving the safety of their cave.

"Okay," Rylie said slowly, "what do you suggest we do?"

Charlie stood and carefully tested her ankle. "We have to draw them out of that underground hideout, maybe with a diversion. Then one of us can go in and get him."

"So one of us will be bait?" Rylie was horrified. "If that's your plan then we need to come up with another one."

Charlie levelled him with a dry look. "I'm not saying one of us will be bait. I just said that we need a diversion. That could be anything. A trap going off, or a fire or something."

Rylie's brows rose in surprise. "Hey, that's not a bad idea. What if we lure them into their own booby-traps?"

Charlie smiled, starting to look a little more enthused. "Now you're talking. Let's cover up the ones we came across yesterday and see if we can find a few more. Maybe we could relocate the simple ones so that they're in a place the pirates aren't expecting."

Rylie bit his lower lip and contemplated. For the first time they had a plan that was within the realm of possible. Admittedly, it was harebrained, however time was of the essence. If Charlie's father hadn't been ransomed, then his days were numbered.

~

Groups returned to their search areas and thankfully for the rest of the day there were no more injuries, although several more traps had been located. It was nearing dusk when the teams were recalled. Searching the island in the dark was simply not an option.

"Alright," Lieutenant Donnelly spoke above the roar of cascading water, "we'd better step up the pace. We have half an hour of daylight left if we're lucky."

Both Ollie and Joey turned from the magnificent view of a waterfall tumbling wildly into a ravine roughly fifteen metres deep. Mist rose from the base of the falls and the water rushed downstream around a bend and disappeared.

THIEF IN THE NIGHT

The forest rose majestically on both sides of the gorge intertwined with vines and thick undergrowth, making visibility beyond its forbidding stand impossible. It was like something out of a movie.

They had crossed the river upstream above the falls to search inland and were now returning.

"This place is incredible." Rifle in her hands, Joey drank in the tropical scenery. "I'm glad I didn't miss this."

Ollie smiled in understanding. Although he had been upset by what had happened to Corey, he had made it clear there was no way he wanted to be back on board the Hartfield away from the action. They all lived for this.

Lieutenant Donnelly had a slightly different opinion. The scenery was indeed remarkably beautiful, but it was a haven for deadly men who thought nothing of setting lethal traps all over the north side of the island. He wanted to get out of here as soon as possible.

"Come on you two." He nodded in the direction of the beach, which was at least twenty minutes away. "We don't want to be caught here in the dark."

~

Charlie and Rylie crouched amidst colourful foliage, large waxy green leaves and thick undergrowth. They held their breath as three pairs of feet slunk stealthily past their hiding place not three paces away. They could see only legs. One set was wearing army camouflage trousers. The other two were in grubby black cotton. Where were the two missing pirates? Perhaps back at the underground hideout? Neither terrified teenager was sure.

They had started out on their self-appointed mission, managing to cover the pit that had spikes protruding at the bottom, which Rylie had nearly fallen into the day before. They had walked another five minutes toward the river and crossed above the falls. Only a few steps into the forest on the other side they had heard rustling leaves and had quickly hidden.

The three men passed stealthily by. Charlie chanced a peek through the undergrowth at their broad retreating backs. Their automatic weapons were to their shoulders and their eyes swept the forest for movement. She looked to Rylie in surprise and he shrugged, just as baffled as she was. They were hunting, but the question was for who? Was someone else on the island?

Charlie beckoned with her hand for Rylie to follow her. Keeping low to the ground, she crept toward the river on a course adjacent to the pirates, unwilling to let them out of her sight.

The men reached the river and fanned out to the right toward the falls. Charlie hunkered down on her belly and crawled to the edge of the jungle, peering out from behind thick vine leaves. Her jaw dropped and her heart raced as she spotted three soldiers crossing the river downstream, each fully armed.

One was a short Asian woman with her long black hair in a ponytail, and the other two were tall men with distinctly western features and light coloured skin. They weren't native to the Pearl Isle.

She gestured furiously for Rylie to crawl forward and take a look. With a confused frown, he complied. His eyes widened in excitement. Charlie's heart plummeted with fear. This was who the pirates were after!

No!

There was nothing she could do to prevent the inevitable. Gunfire suddenly rained down upon the soldiers from the jungle.

23

Bullets whizzed past Lieutenant Donnelly's ears and he automatically shouldered his weapon and fired into the area where they seemed to be coming from. There was no cover in the middle of the river where they were waist deep, and so he backed toward the riverbank behind them as he fired. Ollie and Joey did the same.

The returned gunfire must have caused their attackers to duck their heads, which bought them enough time to reach the side they had just come from. Ollie was backing into the trees with Joey only a step behind him providing cover fire, while Joshua turned and rushed toward the bank.

He was two paces away when automatic fire from across the river ripped into them like a barrage of angry wasps. He jerked, twisted and went down with a splash.

Ollie let out a yelp of pain as a bullet drove hard into his left knee, shattering and dislodging bone. He fell, partially sheltered by leafy vines and low shrubbery. Joey felt something bite into the side of her head, which offset her balance and she landed on her backside.

She frantically searched the water for the lieutenant. She spotted his body, face up but unconscious, being pulled by the current toward the falls. Was he dead?

Without thought, she dove into the water amidst a continual spray of bullets and lunged for him. Her hands gripped his flak jacket and did not let go, even when she lost her footing and the current whisked them along.

The river beneath them suddenly disappeared and she felt them both falling. She drew a deep breath seconds before plunging into the raging depths below.

The water pummelled, churned and then spat them out. Still her hands did not let go. She surfaced behind the cascading flow gasping for breath. Her right hand clung to the XO's vest while she reached for the rock shelf a few feet away with her left.

She kicked hard and managed to get a grip on a piece of rock jutting from the shelf in the small cavern behind the falls. She struggled onto the ledge with her legs and free hand, still tightly clutching Joshua's flak jacket to keep his head above water.

The adrenalin and panic pumping through her fuelled her actions and she managed to drag him onto the ledge beside her. He did not move. Was he dead?

She swallowed a sob and shook him violently. His confused eyes came open and he began coughing. Joey sagged with relief and sat back, watching as he rolled onto his stomach, coughed some more and groaned.

"What happened?" He gasped.

Joey scowled as though it had been his fault. "You just went over a waterfall, that's what happened."

He coughed again as his lungs rejected river water and he glanced at her sitting beside him. "And so did you by the looks of it."

"Where did you get hit?" His flak jacket had saved his life.

"Right in the middle of my back." He winced and slowly sat up. "It must have knocked me unconscious."

Joey worried there might be broken ribs or internal bleeding. "Want me to take a look?"

He stared at the water pouring down before them as though he could see through it if he tried hard. "Where's Ollie?"

"He was on the riverbank. He got hit and then something bit me. I saw you floating toward the falls and dove in to get you and then, well... Here we are." She shrugged, an action belying how she truly felt.

Her hands were shaking and her heart was hammering against her ribcage. Joshua's intense gaze swung to her.

"Something bit you? Where?"

She was just beginning to become aware of a stinging sensation above her left ear. "My head."

Alarm seemed to hit him almost as hard as the bullet that had ploughed into his back. His eyes searched her face and hair until they rested upon a trail of crimson trickling past her left ear and down her neck.

Joey was sitting close enough so that he was able to take her jaw gently in his hand. He turned her head so that the light from outside the cavern shone fully upon the wound. She heard him exhale with relief.

"You've had a close call with a bullet. Thankfully it's just a graze. An inch more and you'd be dead."

He released her and they stared at one another, each taking in the full import of their situation. Ollie was injured or could very well be dead and they had no way of getting to him.

The falls had robbed them of their rifles and waterlogged their radios, but thankfully they still had their side arms which were secure in holsters strapped to their waists.

Nevertheless, in order to get out they would have to survive the turbulent river, scale a fifteen metre cliff and then face armed pirates at the top. The odds were not looking good.

~

Charlie watched two of the soldiers disappear over the falls and the third drag himself out of view into the jungle as a hail of gunfire continued to shower down upon him mercilessly. She had to help.

Before she could think of what to do, Rylie made an uncharacteristic move by charging across the river. They were upstream and yet still in view of the pirates. Panicked and not wanting to be left behind, she sprinted after him.

Gunfire turned from the soldiers and pinged into the water around the teenagers.

"God, protect us please?" she heard Rylie plead over and over again as they waded hastily across the river.

Yes, God, if You really are there please do what he says?

Rylie crawled onto the bank on the other side and turned around, stretching his hand toward her. She reached for it. His strong fingers latched onto her wrist and he pulled her onto the bank beside him. With bullets splintering the trees around their heads, they dove into the cover of heavy undergrowth.

"Come on." Rylie belly crawled a little deeper into the forest.

The gunfire stopped. They were out of view. It would not be long before the pirates decided to pursue. Charlie came to her feet at the same time Rylie did and they ran downstream. Charlie had no fear of booby-traps, having already scouted the area, they knew where they were.

The sound of shouting and splashing caused Charlie's heart to leap into her throat.

They're crossing!

The alarming realisation caused her to speed up. Rylie kept pace behind her, pushing vines and leaves aside, dodging trees and leaping over protruding roots. Suddenly Rylie stopped and she ground to a halt, breathing hard.

"This is the spot," he whispered and forced his lungs to draw breath quietly. "He must be here somewhere."

Charlie's ears picked up a noise ahead to their left. Daylight was beginning to recede and she strained to focus. She waited and it came again. It was the sound of something dragging through leaves and undergrowth.

"He's over there." She pointed ahead and slightly to their left.

Behind them twigs snapped and leaves rustled loudly as the pirates pursued them at full speed. The two teens broke into a run toward the area Charlie had pointed out. Suddenly a rifle bolt snapped shut.

They froze.

"Whoever you are don't shoot!" Rylie hissed, his eyes scanning the undergrowth for the soldier they knew was hiding. "We're just two kids."

"Over there." Charlie pointed again. She darted an anxious glance behind them and then back to the spot not three metres directly in front of them.

A rifle muzzle peered over the top of a fallen tree. The trunk was old and rotting and just above the barrel was a pair of grey, hunted eyes. Strands of brown hair fell across a perspiring brow. The rifle disappeared over the other side of the log and so did the eyes.

The sound of pirates crashing through the jungle behind them spurred them forward. They both scaled the log and dropped down on the other side. Lying behind it was the injured soldier, breathing hard with the agony he had to be feeling from a bullet that had clearly shattered his knee. Grey eyes clouded by pain regarded them in bewilderment.

"Who are you?" he asked in a hoarse whisper.

Charlie looped one of the injured man's arms around her shoulder. "There'll be time for introductions later."

Rylie took the gun, quickly slung it over his shoulder and then grabbed the man's other arm. Between the two of them, they dragged him to his feet.

"Let's take him to the cave."

"We'll never make it that far," Charlie whispered back, listening to the undergrowth crackle under rushing feet. The pirates were growing closer.

"No, but we'll make it to the pit. It's getting dark and they might not see it," he hissed back and started them in that direction.

"We might not see it either."

The soldier clenched his jaw and gritted his teeth to keep from screaming as he was practically dragged at a jog through the forest. Suddenly Rylie dropped to the earth, taking the injured man and Charlie with him. He stifled a cry as they all landed on their stomachs and his injured knee hit the dirt.

Around them large trees reached for the sky and stretched their leaves over them like a protective covering.

"Where is it?" Charlie asked softly.

"Just behind us to our right. It's smack in the middle of the walking trail they're following."

The sound of rushing footsteps ceased and the jungle was eerily silent. They were being hunted.

Charlie could imagine the pirates' slow, deliberate steps, their weapons to their shoulders ready to shoot. Her eyes adjusted to the dim light and through the undergrowth she could just make out the pit, and then only because a small piece of netting was protruding from the carpet of leaves she and Rylie had covered it with earlier. Would the pirates notice?

The soldier lying beside her was breathing heavily. A twig snapped nearby and she quickly clamped her hand over his mouth, her eyes locking with his and pleading with him to be even quieter.

Obviously in a sea of agony, he forced his breathing to even out. The tendrils of pain shooting out from his knee must have reached their pinnacle, as he passed out. His breathing dropped to an almost silent noise level and fear spiralled through Charlie. Was he dead?

She removed her hand and glanced across at Rylie on the other side of the unconscious man in alarm. He shook his head and held a finger to his lips.

Keep quiet, Charlie, or we'll all be dead.

Her gaze returned to the rough-hewn trail to her right and she spotted them. A pair of grubby feet stepped stealthily into view. Behind them was a second pair and then a third. The first was only a few inches from the pit.

One more step, just one more step.

The right foot raised, moved forward and came down slowly. The net gave way and the first rogue let out a scream as he lost his balance and fell in. Charlie squeezed her eyes shut tightly, knowing the fate he had come to.

The second pair of feet halted and one of the men let out a yelp of surprise. The other cursed bitterly. Both pairs of feet moved tentatively to the edge of the exposed pit.

"Sadewa's dead."

"And we'll be too if we keep going," the other replied, fear evident in his voice. "There's no way we can navigate the snares in the dark."

"But they are out there!"

"They are kids and the man is wounded. The other two are dead. Besides, there are more of them on the island and our gunfire will draw them here. We are better off hiding underground and letting the traps take them tonight."

There was an uncomfortable pause and then one set of bare feet turned and started back toward the river. The second followed.

"We will come back at first light."

Charlie heard the comment as the men began to jog toward their hideout. She sighed and glanced across at Rylie.

He dropped his forehead to the earth in relief. "Thank You God!"

"I'm with you." She grinned at the surprised expression he directed her way.

He smiled broadly and they got to their feet. Wordlessly they lifted the unconscious soldier and carried him to the cave, and safety.

24

Elizabeth Hunter sat in the comfortable chair she had drawn to the large window in their suite at the resort. The full moon cast its brilliance across Crystal Bay as it rose higher in the velvet black sky.

Her troubled gaze looked out over yachts and fishing vessels alike, bobbing gently in water that was glittering as though covered with a million small diamonds. However it was not the beauty outside that occupied her thoughts.

Behind her Ezekiel stirred in bed. She glanced his way and saw his eyes open. He squinted against the moonlight pouring into the room and sat up. He rubbed his weary face and swung his legs over the edge of the bed. He stood and covered the short distance between them, placing his hand on her shoulder.

"Can't sleep?"

She looked up pensively. "Zeke, God wouldn't put Rylie so heavily upon my heart to pray for him if he was dead, would He?"

He studied her intuitively. "Are you sure it's God or is it worry?"

"It's God, I'm sure of it."

"Then no, I guess He wouldn't."

The couple stared out the window in silence for several minutes, each deep in thought. Elizabeth finally broke the stillness.

"I've such a burden for him. He's going through something difficult. I can sense the Holy Spirit's urging within me to pray."

"Let's do it together." Ezekiel squeezed her shoulder and lowered stiffly to his knees on the carpet beside her chair.

She joined him there and together they lifted earnest prayers for their son.

~

"Captain, there's rapid gunfire further inland," Lon transmitted from his place beside one of the two RHIBs. "Every team has returned except for the XO's. Requesting permission to do a reconnaissance inland to find them."

"Granted," Commander Kelly's voice returned through Lon's earpiece. "Be careful and stay in contact."

"Yes sir." Lon gestured with a wave of his arm for Graham Steele and Ryan Blackwell to follow him. "Wilko, Wes and Katie come with me," he transmitted to the group in sight, but far enough down the beach to be out of hearing range.

Two teams were there with the other RHIB, waiting for the all clear to return to the ship.

"Farmer," he transmitted again to the group down the beach. "We're leaving Coz here at the RHIB. Would you bring up the other RHIB and keep watch with him? I want you to stick together."

"Roger that. Have you got torches to see so you don't set off any more traps?"

Lon held the button clipped to his vest down. "Torchlight will give away our position. We should be alright with just moonlight. It's bright and we know where most of the traps are now."

"Be careful."

"We will."

Lon sent up a silent plea for help to his new Commander. The jungle loomed tall, dark and still. It was the silence that scared him. Had the lieutenant, Ollie and Joey survived the gun battle?

Another minute passed and Wilko, Wes and Katie arrived at the RHIB, having jogged. Down the beach the second RHIB's engine burbled to life. Lon and his team of five set off into the trees to find out what had become of their comrades.

~

Darkness had fallen, although the landscape was dimly lit by a full moon filtering through the heavy jungle. Inside the cavern behind the waterfall it was completely black.

The lieutenant and Joey sat huddled together, both wet and a little chilled. With the sun's decline, the humidity had swiftly departed from the air. The temperature could not be described as frigid, certainly not in summer in the tropics, but it was decidedly cool.

Joey was impatient to get out and look for Ollie. "Do you suppose they're gone?"

"I certainly hope so. It's my guess they'll think we're dead."

He did not mention that the pirates would have gone after Ollie. That was a given. However, had he and Joey tried to escape immediately it would have been a suicidal effort. Hopefully their shipmate had hidden himself somewhere and radioed for backup.

"How are we going to get out of here?" Joey's voice came through the darkness.

"I've been thinking about that. We'll have to float downstream. This gorge can't go all that far and the river is bound to flatten out and slow down."

"And if we encounter another waterfall?"

Joshua was silent. He had thought of that too. Yet they certainly couldn't wait to be rescued. No one knew they were there. In fact, the crew of the Hartfield would search for them downstream, probably expecting to find their bodies.

"Joshua?"

He noticed her break with protocol and heard the anxiety in her tone. "Yes?"

A small hand slipped into his and held on tightly. His fingers closed around hers and his heart squeezed with an undefined emotion.

She did not immediately speak, causing him to wonder if she was debating whether to say what was really on her mind.

"What is it?"

"Have you ever given a thought to God?"

Joshua frowned in bewilderment. Where had that come from? "Not really. Why?"

"Do you believe He exists?"

What he wouldn't give to be able to look into her face in that moment. He turned her direction regardless. "Sure I do."

"And what about Jesus, do you ever give Him much thought?"

Joshua was extremely curious. "No, I don't. My wife went to church and got into religion not long after we were married, but I never went along."

"Why not?"

"I guess I just wasn't interested."

There was silence for a full minute before Joey decided to be blunt. "Josh, if I hadn't pulled you out of the water, you would have drowned today."

He smiled and squeezed her hand. "Then we're even."

"You don't understand." Anguish had filled her voice.

"You're right," he admitted, a bit baffled, "I don't. Why is this so important to you?"

She reached out in the darkness and rested her free hand upon his arm. That and her small hand in his impacted him more than he ever imagined it would.

"You're not ready to die. You haven't given God the time of day and you haven't realised that you sin and that sin has a cost. Jesus died to take the punishment for your wrongdoing so that you can have a close relationship with God. Without accepting that sacrifice as a gift and choosing to put Him in charge of your life, you're destined for a lost eternity.

"Don't get me wrong, I'm not saying that I am sinless and oh so perfect. Not for one second! I'm just forgiven and I know you need that too. I can't stand the thought of losing you forever. If I feel that way and I'm only human, imagine how God feels!" Joey's free hand slid from his arm and she withdrew the hand holding his.

He felt strangely bereft without her touch. He was also stunned speechless. Every word she had spoken had struck him like a blow. Could it be true? But he had lived a good, moral life. Surely that was all God expected?

"Good deeds and moral choices are not enough."

Now that was uncanny. How had she known that was what he was thinking?

"You only have to be born to be tainted by sin. It's in every one of us, from a selfish thought, to a harsh word or an unkind deed."

Without warning Joshua's mind returned to a conversation he'd had with his wife only weeks before her death.

"I don't get why you need Jesus," he commented one morning after she had returned from church. "I love you. Isn't that enough?"

Amanda's lovely green eyes regarded him soberly across the kitchen table as they sat down to lunch. "No, sweetheart, it isn't."

Her reply, although gentle, cut him to the heart and he did not know how to respond. His hurt and confusion must have been obvious, for she calmly went on to explain.

"As powerfully as you love me, Joshua, it won't stop me from dying when it's my time. When that happens, I'll have to face God and answer for every thought, word and deed I've ever had and done.

"Your love can't wash me clean of my sins, of the things that separate me from God. You see, there's a greater love we're all made for, the love of our Creator. Without it there will always be a sense of restlessness and longing. If you're honest with yourself, my love can't satisfy you either."

For the first time he listened as she explained God's plan in sending Jesus Christ His son to the earth. Something inside him stirred with the longing she spoke of. He quickly shoved it aside. He was a good person. Only criminals and really bad people needed the sacrifice Jesus had made on the cross. Not him and certainly not Amanda!

He closed the conversation rather abruptly when he said as much. And yet as he rose hastily from the table, some-

thing in her expression gripped his heart. It was obvious she disagreed and anxiety caused tears to pool in her eyes.

He left the kitchen quickly and headed for his shed to work for a time, however long it would take to rid his memory of that look of loving concern on her beautiful face.

The memory arose vividly and Joshua felt that same longing now that he had experienced when she talked of God's greater love. If Joey was right about God requiring him to account for even his thoughts, then he was surely guilty and his wife had been correct.

"But why would He want me when I've lived my life without Him and never given Him a moment's thought?"

"Because He has a father's love for you," Joey replied with an earnestness he had never heard before. "You were never able to meet your son and get to know him, but I'll bet you would give your life for him if you could."

The analogy struck a chord deep within him and tears sprang to his eyes. "I would."

"And that's exactly what He did for you."

The roar of the waterfall filled the cavern and yet in his heart, Joshua was quiet. His mind was filled with a picture of a wooden cross upon which an innocent Man was nailed to its brutal beams. A flicker of faith flamed within him. He believed.

God, I'm sorry for living my life without You, and I'm sorry for the things I've done that put Your Son on that cross. I invite You to be in charge of my life from now on.

A void he hadn't even known he possessed was suddenly filled to overflowing, spilling abundant joy and a love so pure and measureless into every crevice of his being. A slow smile crept over his face.

"Joshua?"

The uncertainty in Joey's voice reminded him of her presence. He drew the remarkable woman beside him into a reassuring embrace.

"You're right. Thank you, Joey, for caring enough to say those hard words."

"But you still disagree?"

He grinned and gave her a squeeze. "On the contrary."

25

Charlie and Rylie managed to cram the unconscious soldier into the small cave they now called home. They gently laid him on the ground, with his torso upright against a large rock near the cave wall. His head rolled back as though on a pillow.

Rylie removed the semi automatic rifle from over his shoulder and propped it by the far wall. He then tore away the blood-soaked material at the man's left knee and screwed up his face at what he saw.

"What a mess!" He sat back and wiped perspiration from his brow with his sleeve.

Charlie scooted to his side and studied the wound. It would need surgery, there was no doubt about that. "What can we do to stop the bleeding?"

Rylie quickly unbuttoned his shirt. He then began to tear the thin cotton into strips. "Here, use some of this to pad the hole and then wrap strips around it like a bandage."

Hesitating with a grimace of distaste for only a moment, Charlie quickly got to work.

"Not too tight or you'll cut off his circulation, but firm enough to add pressure that will stop the bleeding." Rylie ripped into his sleeves at the seams and placed them in a pile nearby.

Charlie glanced at them curiously. "What are those for?"

"We'll need to make some sort of splint so that we don't

make the injury worse when we move him around. I'll be back in a few minutes."

He stood and walked hunched over to the entrance so that his head would not bang against the roof of the small cavern.

Charlie glanced up in anxious surprise. "Where are you going?"

"To get something we can use for splints."

"Okay," she reluctantly agreed and watched him go.

She then finished wrapping the wound and tucked the end of the 'bandage' under itself so that it would not unravel. She sat back and studied the injured man.

He was tall, as evidenced by his long legs stretching before him. Strands of brown hair fell across his forehead which was smudged with dirt and blood. His hands also were covered in scarlet. She supposed when he was clean he would be very handsome.

He wore a dark navy coloured flak jacket and a belt upon which hung a pistol in its holster. His camouflage trousers and shirt were not the usual army green. Instead they were a mixture of dark blue and grey. On his shoulders were rank stripes and upon his upper arm an insignia patch. He wasn't army. He was navy.

The pirates had said there were more on the island. They had meant there were more navy personnel. Why had they come? Clearly they were after the pirates. Were they here to rescue her father? She assumed so and felt a burden lift from her shoulders. She knew it was too big a task for her and Rylie. She had been deluding herself all along.

The shrubbery covering the entrance rustled and then moved aside as her accomplice squeezed in. He rearranged the foliage to hide it again and crossed to the unconscious sailor. He placed two straight thick sticks on the ground one either side of the wound. Without speaking, he and Charlie worked together to carefully bind the splints to the injured leg.

They were just finishing the task when the sailor groaned and his head rolled from left slowly to the centre. His eyes opened and he blinked, staring at the cave ceiling in confusion. His rescuers exchanged pleased glances.

Charlie smiled. "I think it's time now for introductions."

The sailor's head came up in surprise and he studied the two teenagers, one either side of him.

"The XO..." His eyes widened in remembrance and he sat up straighter and winced with terrible pain. He leaned back against the rock. "Joey."

"Was that the other two navy people with you?"

Rylie's expression quirked in bewilderment. "Navy? I thought he was army."

Charlie pointed out the insignia patch on the man's upper shirt arm, answering as though he was not sitting there listening to them. "Nope. He's navy."

Rylie glanced back at the sailor and grinned. "Cool."

"Lieutenant Donnelly, Joey... Where are they?" The man's jaw tensed as he fought wave upon wave of pain shooting up his leg.

Charlie and Rylie exchanged sober glances.

Charlie dreaded being the bearer of bad news. "Do you tell him or do I?"

Rylie's face filled with compassion as he looked into the sailor's clouded eyes. He already knew. "The man got shot and he floated down the river like he was dead and the girl jumped in to get him just after you got hit. They both went over the waterfall."

The injured man's head dropped back against the rock and he swallowed hard against the lump forming in his throat.

"They could have survived," Rylie offered hopefully. "Those vests you're wearing are bulletproof, right? He might have gotten hit in the vest. The woman, Joey, might have been able to save him."

The sailor did not appear so optimistic. An uncomfortable silence settled. Rylie looked to Charlie in desperation, his eyes pleading for help. What could they say to offer comfort? Charlie opted to change the subject.

"I'm Charlotte Mickleson and this is Rylie Hunter." She gestured to her companion.

The sailor's head snapped back up and he regarded them in astonishment. "You're alive?"

Charlie's brows shot upward. "You were looking for us?"

A half smile tugged at the man's lips. "Yeah. Where is your father?" Without waiting for an answer, he turned to Rylie. "And how did you escape the shack on the island?"

Rylie was just as stunned. "You know about that?"

"Yeah, we found it the day before yesterday. We also caught Zacutti."

"Who?" he and Charlie chimed together.

"Black hair and dark eyes, creepy tattoo of a skull on his face..."

Rylie visibly shuddered. "Yeah, that's him."

"Tell me what happened."

"What's your name first?" Charlie chipped in curiously.

He exhaled, shifted slightly to get comfortable and grimaced. "Ollie."

Rylie smiled. "Nice to formally meet you, Ollie. Hey, is

there any way you can contact your ship?"

Ollie touched his ear and cheek and growled under his breath. "Of all the stupid..." He then felt his vest looking for something. He reached with his right hand to his left shoulder blade. The pocket there was empty.

"What's wrong?"

The teenagers exchanged confused glances again.

Ollie exhaled in frustration. "My radio and headset are gone. It must have snagged on something and fallen out back there."

Rylie sagged in disappointment.

Charlie was regretful but pragmatic. "I'm thinking that's not good."

Rylie snorted. "That's an understatement."

"Well," she said dryly, "I guess we've got time to tell you what happened."

Ollie winced as he shifted to get comfortable. "I guess."

Rylie's eyes sparkled wickedly. "Just be wary when she makes herself out to be the hero."

Charlie sent him a scowl, directed her attention to their captive audience and gathered her dignity about her. She then began to tell their tale with animated gestures.

~

"The money coming into his accounts was difficult to track. It was carefully laundered through a variety of legitimate businesses."

Paul Jensen, the head of the federal police department, listened to Dylan with interest. The man was one of his best. Paul stared out his office window overlooking glassy high-rise buildings winking in the late sunlight.

"We were finally able to locate its original source. Also, the man we have in custody, Zacutti, who is being transported to us from the Pearl Islands, has talked. He seems to be the go between, carrying out the groundwork for Pritchard. He has been distributing the drugs to biker gangs once they hit Australian soil."

"As well as being Pritchard's henchman." Paul was thinking of the kidnappings. "So, do we have the evidence we need to pay Mr. Pritchard a visit and offer him accommodation in one of Australia's finest detention centres?"

"We do."

Paul nodded with satisfaction. "Excellent."

"I have a man in the Islands now, Jack Coleman. I've instructed him to drop by Blue Jay Island to collect another passenger for the flight back to the mainland."

Paul smiled broadly. "One Mr. Alexander Pritchard, I presume."

"That would be the one."

26

"Okay, so what's the plan again?" Joey dropped into the water behind the falls with her hands clinging to the rock ledge.

This is ludicrous!

Joshua slid in beside her. "We ride the current until we get to a spot where the gorge isn't so steep, then we climb out."

"Have I mentioned that I'm not a brilliant swimmer?" She was no longer wearing her vest, but even that would not be enough.

Joshua could not resist a smile. "You plucked me from the river didn't you?"

"Not really, I just didn't let go. Besides, I had a ledge to hang on to."

Joey's uncertain, half moon shaped eyes stared through the water cascading before them. Already the current was tugging at her, desiring to pull her under its powerful downpour and spit her out into a roiling mass of river.

"Give me a break, Able Seaman." Joshua's voice held a teasing note. "You're fearless. You got straight back on the job after you were kidnapped. You walked into Zacutti's quarters and told him to his face that you'd forgiven him, and less than an hour ago you leapt over a waterfall to save my neck."

Joey was surprised. "You know about what I said to Zacutti?"

Joshua chuckled. "Are you kidding? You threw Wilko for a

six! He wouldn't shut up about it. Everyone on board knows."

Joey let the matter drop. All she could think about was drowning and what a terrible experience it had been. She did not want to go through that again. Worse yet, this time there would be no one to pull her from the water. Joshua might very well drown with her. That thought alone was horrific. As panic was rising within her, so too was a Scripture that she now knew by heart.

'Who can find a virtuous woman? For her price is far above rubies.'

Virtuous, a woman of valour.

Joey took a deep breath, sent a prayer for help winging toward heaven and pushed away from the ledge. "Let's ride this thing!"

She was swiftly sucked under the falls. The water spilling into the gorge from above pummelled her against the rocky river bottom before violently tossing her into the mad fray on the other side. She surfaced gasping for air, only to have the strong current pull her down stream in a wild fight for her life.

Large boulders lay beneath the surface. The river rushed over them swiftly, churning up white foam. Joey gasped when her head breached the surface again, only to be sucked under by the current and thrust into a boulder. Her right hip smarted from the impact but she dared not cry out lest she draw in a lungful of water.

She clawed for the surface, managed another breath and was then whisked under as the river flowed past two large rocks on either side into a dip. The moonlight failed to illumi-nate the river bottom and all she saw was blackness. Panic rose within her but she forced it back. She had to think rationally now or drown.

Something crashed into her and then whooshed past. She realised too late that is was the lieutenant. The collision spun her one-hundred and eighty degrees, straight into another submerged boulder. A sharp edge dug into her left shoulder, tearing her shirt and biting into her skin.

The current mercilessly pulled her onward, giving no quarter. Her lungs screamed for oxygen. Another rise between submerged boulders caused her to bob to the surface where she quickly drew a breath before being dunked in the next dip.

She swirled in the vortex and was spun out into the current again. Her eyes caught a blurry glimpse of the moon above the trees before blackness once again engulfed her. The churning river tossed her against a large rock poking its enormous head above the water centre stream, and her fingernails chipped and snapped as she clawed for a handhold. Joey gasped for breath as water rushed past her ears and pulled her in its powerful clutches toward her death.

Suddenly a large hand reached from seemingly nowhere and grasped the back of her collar in a death grip. It dragged her like a waterlogged cat onto the rock. She was too busy coughing and spluttering at first to take any notice of the body that now sat beside her.

Finally when her lungs had rejected the last drop of water, she moved from her stomach to her hands and knees and then onto her backside.

"You alright?" Joshua sounded winded.

"Yeah, but no more late night swims in the moonlight, okay?"

He chuckled and rose stiffly to his feet. Joey's hip was

sending out complaints and her shoulder was hurting something fierce. She gingerly fingered the large tear near her shoulder blade and was not surprised to feel warm dark liquid issuing from a nasty gash. Knowing they were not out of this predicament yet, she chose to ignore it.

Her gaze followed the lieutenant's up the steep gorge wall close by on their left. Although its height was still at least fifteen metres, it did not seem to be a sheer drop as it was near the falls. Here rocks were jutting out that would provide sufficient hand holds, and the wall was inclined several degrees toward the jungle.

Joey felt confident as she studied the rough surface. "I can climb this."

Joshua studied the cliff with a frown. "Well it seems that's our only choice." He turned to her with a mischievous gleam in his eyes. "Unless you want to go for another late night swim."

She grinned. "Not on your life, sir! I'll go up first."

"Alright, just be careful once you get to the top. Those men might still be around."

"That being the case, we'd better get out of here. We're sitting ducks."

"I know."

Joey surveyed the one metre gap between the boulder they were on and the gorge wall. Thankfully it was slightly inclined and large rock formations were protruding. She moved to the edge of the boulder and positioned her feet securely.

Refusing to look at the water gushing between the wall and the boulder, she leapt. Her feet lost their footing when she crashed against the wall, but her hands found a solid grip on a small rock shelf. The river tugged at her boots that were dipped in its current. Her wet hands were slipping.

In the bright moonlight she was able to see a larger chunk of rock jutting from the wall to her right. She reached for it with her right leg unsuccessfully twice before finally gaining a solid foothold. She was then able to reach with her right hand to a higher handhold.

Remembering pleasurable days of climbing the large oak tree in her backyard as a child, she methodically made her way upward until at last dirt and leaves met her fingertips. Using an overhanging tree root, she pulled herself onto solid ground.

She warily swept the jungle around her with keen eyes and carefully listened for any sign of unwanted company. Satisfied they were alone, she glanced back down at the lieutenant who made the same leap and began to climb. His larger boots struggled to find sufficient footholds which made the task difficult.

Joey grabbed a thick vine hanging from the tree above her and gave it a sound yank. With some difficulty, she freed it from the tree, wrapped it once around the trunk so that she would be able to support the lieutenant's weight and dangled the end over the gorge.

Joshua gave it a tug to test its reliability and then used it to pull himself up the rest of the way. Finally he crawled onto the forest floor and dropped down beside Joey. It had been a long day and they were both exhausted. But it wasn't over yet.

~

Rylie sat across the cavern leaning against the wall watching the sailor opposite him. Ollie's head rolled back and forth as he muttered in his sleep. His brow was beaded with sweat and his complexion was extremely pale.

Rylie's mind returned to that terrifying moment over an hour ago when one of the pirates had fallen in the pit and the other two had discussed their options.

"Sadewa's dead."

"And we'll be too if we keep going. There is no way we can navigate the snares in the dark."

"But they are out there," the first argued hotly.

"They are kids and the man is wounded. The other two are dead. Besides, there are more of them on the island and our gunfire will draw them here. We are better off hiding underground and letting the traps take them tonight."

There was an uncomfortable pause and then one set of feet turned and started back toward the river. The second followed.

"We will come back at first light."

Rylie's mind played one phrase over and over again.

"... there are more of them on the island..."

Ollie needed help and the pirates had gone underground. Now was their chance to go for help. His gaze shifted to Charlie curled into a tight ball on the floor fast asleep. A plan began to formulate in his alert mind. It was frightening, but also viable.

He wanted to shy away from the challenge and simply hide here until it was all over. However, if he did nothing, this nightmare would never end and the pirates would shed more innocent blood. It was time for action.

He crawled across the cavern and shook the sailor. Ollie's eyes came open with a start and he jerked awake.

"It's okay," Rylie whispered and the sailor's pain clouded gaze came to rest on him. He calmed. "I'm going for help."

Ollie's brain cleared of sleep and he frowned at Rylie crouching beside him. "No, it's not safe."

"It's a whole lot safer now than it will be in the morning when those pirates come out of their hideout. Will you loan me your bullet proof vest?"

Ollie's dubious eyes took in the boy's bare chest and his gaze dropped to the shirt strips binding his knee. A touch of guilt entered his grey eyes. "Here," he said as he shed his vest and then his camouflage top, "take my shirt as well." Beneath it he still wore a standard navy issue grey t-shirt.

"Thanks." Rylie realised that camouflage was what he needed. In this bright moonlight, his lily-white chest would give him away. He quickly pulled the long sleeve shirt over his head and then donned the vest. Both were rather baggy on him. He was tall but did not have Ollie's muscles to fill them out.

Charlie stirred and sat up. She blinked, rubbed her eyes and stared at him for several silent minutes. It did not take a genius to figure out what he was planning. "I'm coming with you."

Rylie levelled her with a pragmatic stare. "No you're not."

"You can't tell me what to-"

"Someone needs to stay here with Ollie. He can't travel with his knee and he needs medical attention right away. Those men are underground hiding and they won't come back until daylight. Now is my only chance."

Charlie did not look pleased. "And what if you get yourself killed in a booby trap like that pirate earlier?"

Rylie held her gaze calmly. "God has kept me safe this far.

He'll watch over me the rest of the way."

She looked like she wanted to laugh at him, but in the end she didn't. He wasn't naive, and she knew it. They had run across numerous traps and only she had been foolish enough to get caught in them. She could not deny that he had some kind of sixth sense, and after what had happened, she seemed more inclined to agree that it was God. She nodded slowly.

"So what's your plan?"

Rylie moved to the entrance and peered outside. The moon cast its brilliance upon the land, filtering easily down through the trees, reflecting off large leaves and creating shadows that sent shivers up his spine.

He glanced back to explain in a whisper that was easily heard in the silence of the cavern. "I'm going to head for the shore. Ollie's ship should be anchored not far off, and if I'm lucky, I might bump into those inflatable boats he said were there. I'll show Ollie's shipmates where the pirates' hideout is and then bring help to you."

Charlie looked surprised that his plan sounded decent. If the pirates could be taken out of the equation, extracting Ollie from the island would be relatively easy.

"Alright, but be careful. Why don't you take the gun?"

Rylie's gaze landed upon the rifle leaning against the wall even as Ollie lodged his protest.

"He doesn't know how to use it, Charlie. He'd only end up shooting himself." He met Rylie's amused gaze.

"You're right. I'll be back as soon as I can." Without another word, he silently disappeared out the entrance.

~

Charlie watched Rylie go and then studied her patient. His worried gaze was fixed on the spot where he had been.

"He'll be alright," she assured him.

Ollie's uncertain gaze met hers. She only smiled.

"If you'd been with him the last couple of days you'd see what I mean. It's totally trippy, but he's got a sixth sense. I didn't believe in God until I met Rylie. He prays and weird things happen."

Ollie sighed and leaned back against the rock. "Yeah well, he's gunna need all the help he can get."

27

"Do not be ridiculous! Now is the perfect time to scout," Soleh argued, the scar across his face more prominent in the partial lighting of their bunker. "That sailor would have heard what you said when Sadewa fell into the pit. He and those other two were probably hiding close by. He will have radioed his shipmates that we have gone into hiding and they will not be expecting us. We can take them out one at a time, guerrilla style."

Ade's clear blue eyes were shadowed by doubt. "These men are not just local police. They are Australian Navy! They are trained for combat."

Manusama pushed his bandana higher on his brow and seriously contemplated the suggestion. Lemah, ignored them all and menacingly ran the tip of his freshly sharpened blade lightly down the prisoner's cheek, wearing a sadistic grin. His spider tattoo looked frighteningly real in the poor lighting.

Dave Mickleson tensed but held the brigand's gaze with a hard stare. He would not give the man the satisfaction of seeing how terrified he really was. Hope burgeoned now that he knew the navy was on the island! Yet part of him wanted to die, just as Charlotte had. It should have been him. Her drowning was his fault. He never should have brought her on this trip!

"Soleh is right. They will not be expecting us, and unless we take them out, we will never get off this island. They have our boat," Manusama pointed out. "Alright, this is the plan..."

~

"So what do we do now?" Joey whispered.

Joshua was standing beside her, listening intently to the jungle around them at the top of the gorge.

"Ollie will have called for backup. It's my guess the other teams have him already." His alert gaze travelled carefully over every tree and shadow.

She remembered the terrifying attack above the falls. What if the pirates had gotten to him first? "And if they don't?"

"Then we'll need backup to scour the island for him." He glanced at her briefly, his pragmatic tone and even gaze soothing her doubts.

She appreciated his calm, level-headed approach. It inspired confidence.

"The shore is that direction." He pointed across the gorge. "We'll cross above the falls and head back to the RHIBs."

Joey followed Joshua as he silently eased between trees toward the falls further upstream. "Are we stopping where Ollie was shot?"

"We'll have a quick look, but I doubt he'll be there."

They followed the gorge around a bend. Gradually the sound of gushing water crashing into the river below grew louder and more insistent. As they drew closer, a fine mist rising from the falls dampened the cool night air and left a thin film of droplets on the jungle's shiny leaves along the gorge.

The moonlight reflected off the river like cheeky little

twinkles from its happy eyes. Or perhaps on a night like this, it was more like glistening tears. Joey couldn't decide which one it was.

Night was whispering age-old knowledge, declaring the glory and wisdom of its Maker. Yes, happy twinkling eyes indeed. At the same time, she felt its sadness. Nobody seemed to be listening anymore.

A shiver ran down her spine as she recognised the place where the gun battle had transpired. Yes, perhaps they were glistening tears after all.

Joshua knelt by the river's edge a few metres past the falls. Joey stood at his side and watched as he fingered a dark patch amongst the dried leaves and moss that blanketed the jungle floor.

Flashes of the heated battle passed before her mind's eye. "That was where Ollie fell."

There had been no time to think or even to feel anything but a rush of adrenaline, as the hail of gunfire had rained down upon them. Now there was too much time to consider all that had happened. There was time also to second-guess herself. Should she have stayed with Ollie? No, then Joshua would have drowned. Could she have dragged him ashore before going over the falls? Not likely, or she would have done it.

She should have provided assistance and protection for her downed comrade. Had he survived? Even if he had called for backup, those pirates had been a whole lot closer than any of the Hartfield's crew.

Dread dropped like a stone to the bottom of Joey's stomach and her chest felt weighted with guilt. She had left him there. She had left Ollie to die.

"See these drag marks?" Joshua pointed to where leaves and moss had been dislodged.

The trail led into the jungle and he painstakingly followed them. Although bright, the moonlight was not terribly helpful in his effort to follow the trail of blood amidst dense undergrowth. His fingers alighted on something small and distinctly man made judging by its shape and texture. He raised it to the light filtering down through the treetops.

Joey's heart sank.

Joshua ran a frustrated hand through his closely cropped dark hair. "It's Ollie's earpiece."

Joey swallowed hard and uninvited tears sprang to her eyes. They both knew what that meant.

Her attention suddenly diverted as a sound incongruent with the continuous lullaby of jungle noises reached her ears. She automatically reached for her side arm and drew it from its holster. Joshua did the same, which meant he had heard it too. It was coming from upstream. Leaves crunched under soft footfalls and undergrowth rustled as someone passed through.

Joshua beckoned with his fingers for her to follow him. They eased silently through the shrubbery, gently moving aside dangling vines and slipping between tree trunks. He stopped at the edge of the forest where he could safely observe the river without being seen.

Joey waited a few paces behind him, covering the jungle behind them with her alert gaze. Her weapon was aimed steadily toward the sound of an approaching threat a few metres to their right.

They waited, listening to the quiet, careful steps of someone who was obviously on edge. Whoever it was, they were alone. Joey momentarily held her breath when there was absolute silence.

The person had stopped. Why? Had he heard them, or was he merely assessing the river before crossing? Joey hoped and prayed it was the latter.

There was splashing and a tall figure waded into view. Joey studied the man crossing the river. In the moonlight she recognised the Australian navy shirt and bulletproof vest. However, the lean fellow wearing it was a mystery. It wasn't anyone they knew. He had to be wearing Ollie's clothing. It made her blood boil with rage. Was he the one that had killed her comrade?

The mystery man reached the other side of the river and glanced back at the opposite bank. In those few seconds, his face was illuminated by moonlight and the image of those wide, frightened eyes burned into Joey's memory. It wasn't a man. It was a teenage boy.

She gripped Joshua's arm, her stunned eyes following the boy as he entered the jungle on the other side and disappeared from view.

"Sir, that's Rylie Hunter! I remember him from the picture we were all shown. You know, the one we received from the police."

"Yes, I remember it. How did he get here, all the way on the other side of the island?"

"I don't know, but I'd sure like to know how he got Ollie's shirt and vest?"

Joshua motioned for her to follow him with a nod of his head in the direction the boy had taken. They cautiously crossed the river.

A twig snapped and Rylie froze. That eerie sense of fore-boding dropped over him like a dark cloud.

God, please protect me from whoever is-

A shadow lunged at him from behind. Something hard and pointed jabbed into his back once, twice and then a frustrated growl as the blade met with impenetrable Kevlar plating.

He twisted under the weight pinning him to the ground. Moonlight poured down through the canopy above them, allowing him to catch a glimpse of dark, malicious eyes. As the blade came down again, this time aimed for his neck, the image of a spider tattooed to the knife wielding hand became visible.

Another shadow leapt from the trees behind them, grasping the hand with the knife and stopping its deadly descent. A muscled arm clad in camouflage clamped around the pirate's neck, cutting off his air supply and wrenching him backward off Rylie.

The two struggled on the ground, the pirate gripping the knife, and the sailor holding the man's wrist to keep the blade from sinking into his flesh.

Another dark figure appeared and Rylie recognised the Asian woman from the river. Her arm was extended and a handgun was silhouetted against the moonlit backdrop.

"Drop the knife or I'll shoot." Her voice was quiet but deadly. "And you can bet from this range I won't miss."

The pirate glanced up, spotted the pistol and reluctantly ceased struggling. The sailor snatched the knife from his grasp, rolled him roughly onto his stomach and twisted his arms behind his back.

"Joey, can you find something to tie his hands?"

Rylie quickly removed his belt and handed it to the woman. "Here, take this."

Still covering the villain with her weapon, she took the belt with her free hand and passed it to her comrade. He bound the pirate's hands behind his back and roughly jerked him to his feet.

He drew his own pistol and pressed the muzzle into the reprobate's back. Joey strode to Rylie. She took his arm and helped him to his feet.

"Are you okay?"

"Yeah." Rylie brushed leaves from his front and then his trousers. "Ollie's vest saved my life."

Joey shot her teammate a hopeful glance. "You know where Ollie is?"

Rylie looked at the two navy sailors he had thought were dead and silently gave God thanks. "Yeah. Charlie's with him. His knee is all shot up but he's alive."

The sailor frisked the pirate whose vengeful eyes bored into them. "Who's Charlie?"

"Charlotte Mickleson."

Joey's eyebrows winged upward. "The girl that was kidnapped?"

"It's a long story." Rylie felt unnerved by the malevolent stare of the man that had just tried to kill him. "Look, if he is out here, then so are the others." He nodded toward the captive. "There's three of them left and they still have Charlie's dad. Can we get backup and I'll take you to where they're keeping him? Then I'll show you where Ollie and Charlie are hiding."

"Sounds like a good plan to me." The sailor thrust the pirate forward in the direction of the shore.

28

Commander Kelly studied his team upon the shore using the EOD on the bridge of the Hartfield. His shrewd gaze narrowed. He pondered what he would do if he was in the pirates' situation.

His gut instinct told him they would try to get their vessel back, and to do so, they would need either a diversion or to take out any other craft that might pursue them.

"Jaffa."

The radio operator removed his headset and met the captain's thoughtful gaze. "Yes sir?"

"Contact Daz and Jamie and check if they've finished siphoning fuel from the pirate vessel as I asked."

"Yes sir." He did as bidden and within seconds Seaman Jamie Oldham's voice came back over the radio through his headset.

"Affirmative. The fuel has been dumped."

"Good. Inform them I'm sending Coz in the second RHIB for a pickup. I want Jamie and Daz back aboard the Hartfield ASAP. Get onto Coz and relay my order."

"Yes sir." Jaffa complied, all the while frowning in puzzlement, clearly wondering what was the captain up to.

~

Coz had taken the two sailors guarding the pirate vessel back to the Hartfield and returned to the beach, and still they waited on the shore for the recon team. Farmer remained at the helm of the second RHIB, and Coz at the wheel of the first, ready at a moment's notice to fire the engines and speed back to the ship.

Woody crouched low at the bow of the first RHIB, rifle aimed into the trees, his eyes alert and scanning the tree line. Able Seaman Yusef was doing the same in the second boat. Ron was poised at the port side of Farmer's RHIB, rifle in hand, monitoring the opposite direction should unwanted company come from down the beach.

All was eerily silent when Jaffa's voice came through on the radio.

"Farmer, the captain has ordered you to get the men out of the RHIBs and take up positions out of sight on the edge of the forest."

Farmer answered as he grabbed up his rifle and stepped carefully to the front of the boat. "Roger that. Alright boys, the captain wants us to take cover."

The four men leapt from the RHIBs and followed Farmer up the beach and into the trees at a jog. Making eye contact and using hand gestures, he indicated where each of the men should position themselves. With the RHIBs still in view and large leafy fronds for cover, they blended into the jungle and set in to silently wait for their comrades, or whatever trouble the captain seemed to be expecting.

They waited another uneventful fifteen minutes. Coz's eyes began to droop sleepily. He shook his head and blinked in an effort to stay awake. Woody smiled at the sight. Nearby Ron shifted uncomfortably, likely experiencing pins and needles in his legs.

Woody checked his watch. They had been gone at least an hour, maybe more. The gunfire they had heard earlier could not have been more than twenty minutes inland. He supposed it was slow going in the dark, on the lookout for both the enemy and booby traps.

Yusef's stomach growled with hunger and Woody, who was crouched beside him, passed him a silent wide grin. They were all equally famished. He opened his mouth to make a comment and then quickly snapped it shut.

What was that sound? It was close and almost undiscernible. Was it merely the breeze rustling the leaves? He strained to hear. Nothing.

No wait. It came again. It sounded like large fronds brushing gently against something as it passed by. No leaves crunched under footfalls, no sound of breathing gave the enemy away. Woody couldn't even be sure that's who or what it was. Was he hearing things?

Suddenly a loud explosion broke the silence and a fireball leapt into the air above deck on the Hartfield. The angry bright flames lit the patrol boat and the surrounding water for a split second, as would a flash of lightning. It gave way to a lesser glow as a blaze now licked at the vessel. The alarm systems aboard the ship went berserk, and even at this distance, urgent voices could be heard on deck. Ron cursed in surprise and stood, his eyes glued to the ship.

Woody's ears picked up a crisp snap of a twig several metres deeper in the trees and he swung his rifle in that direction, remaining down amidst the undergrowth out of sight. He heard a grunt, not from one of his comrades, and a few seconds later a second explosion rent the night air.

Ron exclaimed and dropped to the ground as the first RHIB went up in a ball of fire and smoke. What was happening?

Woody guessed it was a grenade and kept his eyes trained on the forest. Moonlight filtered down through the canopy and also from the direction of the beach.

Shadows. All he could see was shadows. Frustration mounted. Amidst the noise of the burning RHIB and the ship's alarms, a metallic clink nearly stopped his heart in his chest.

Could that be a pin being pulled from a grenade? He aimed where the sound came from and fired several shots in quick succession. There was a groan of pain and seconds later an-other explosion, this time so close to them that Woody could feel the heat from the blast like an oven against his skin.

He ducked reflexively, face to the ground as a plume of orange balled upward and then died out as quickly as it had come. He could smell singed hair and burning plants.

Beside him Yusef had hit the dirt as well. Coz and Ron stayed down, obviously afraid there would be more gre-nades. Farmer snaked on his belly through the undergrowth toward the sound of another groan and shuffling leaves. Woody followed him for backup. The enemy was finally spotted roughly ten metres away, on his back clutching his right shoulder. How he had managed to hit the guy at all, he would never know.

Rifle to his shoulder, Farmer rose to one knee with the other foot flat on the ground supporting him. "Make one wrong move and I'll pull this trigger."

The pirate moaned, in agony from the shoulder wound and also from the burns he had sustained from the close explo-sion. Woody deducted that he had pulled the pin, been hit in the shoulder by a bullet, and tossed the grenade as he fell. As a result, he hadn't managed to get the distance he had desired from the desperate throw.

"Where are the others?" Farmer demanded.

This was met with another groan.

"Where are they?"

"Alone," the pirate gritted out between clenched teeth. "I am alone."

"I'll believe that when hell freezes over! Scout the area!" he tossed over his shoulder at his men.

Coz and Ron gingerly emerged, and with rifles at their shoulders, began to carefully search to the east and Woody and Yusef to the west.

~

Shep and Switch fought to put out the deck fire. Jaffa, Jamie and Daz scoured the ship for the intruder that had caused it. Meanwhile, the captain maintained communications with his men.

Sabotage. Commander Kelly had warned them it might happen. Despite that, Jamie had still been surprised when he heard a metallic clatter on the deck not far from where he was keeping watch, and then seconds later the explosion.

A grenade. It had to have been a grenade, which meant that the pirate who had thrown it was either close by in the water, or still on board. Spotlights shone on both the deck and the surrounding cove.

"The lower decks are secure." Daz's voice was just above a whisper as he came to a stop beside Jamie on the quarter deck. They were near the davit cradle where the RHIBs were launched. "Jaffa an' me searched everywhere down below and came up with nothing. Whoever did this must have tossed the grenade up and over the side from the water. Anyway, Jaffa's helping Katie and Shep. They've got it pretty much under control now."

Jamie acknowledged him with a glance and a nod as he warily peered over the edge of the quarter deck, handgun barrel pointing wherever his gaze travelled. Nothing.

He had searched every square inch of the deck and upper levels as well as scanning the surrounding ocean with a spotlight. Now he was traversing the deck one more time. Whoever had thrown that grenade was long gone.

He replaced his handgun in its holster and followed Daz to check on the progress with the fire. They would need to assess the damage to the ship's structure and machinery and report to the captain. Jamie wished Wilko was aboard. As chief engineer, that task was in his area of expertise.

~

Joey was walking ahead of Rylie, her gun grasped in both hands aimed somewhere ahead of her feet. Her eyes swept carefully from left to right. Behind her Rylie trode softly through the undergrowth, his every sense alert. Lieutenant Donnelly brought up the rear, the prisoner forced to walk in front of him. One of Joshua's hands gripped his weapon and the other the prisoner's bound wrists.

"Whoever you are, stop right there," a low threatening voice suddenly demanded several metres to Joey's left.

She froze, as did the others behind her. Her gaze snapped in that direction and a split second later she drew from memory that voice. "Lon?"

The bosun stepped from amidst a tangle of vines dangling from an ancient twisted tree trunk. "Able Seaman Shafer?"

Joey let out a relieved breath. "Mate, are we glad to see you! The XO here has one of the pirates, but Rylie says there are three more."

A white toothy grin gleamed in the moonlight as Lon came closer. "Make that two left. Farmer captured one of them when he tried to blast the shore party to pieces. Thankfully everyone is alright, although according to Farmer, the scoundrel they've detained has seen better days. What's this about Rylie?" Lon's gaze passed to the youth standing nervously behind the small chef.

Lieutenant Donnelly stepped forward, his prisoner in a firm grasp in front of him. He grinned. "Petty Officer Lonigan, meet Rylie Hunter."

Lon whistled low in astonishment. "Well I'll be." He studied the boy.

Rylie's nervous gaze shifted from the enormous sailor to the shadows now creeping from amongst the undergrowth to encircle them. There were five, all ranging in stature from large to small, all wearing navy camouflage and all bearing weapons.

"What's the situation report?" Joshua asked the group.

"We were ordered to keep looking for you while the team we left on the beach go after the pirates the captain suspects will try to commandeer their vessel again."

Wilko frowned. "Where's Ollie?"

Before anyone could answer, distant gunfire again disturbed the eerie silence. All heads swivelled toward the shore. Another explosion followed, marked by a plume of raging fire that leapt high into the air.

"That had better not be the last RHIB," Lon grumbled.

Joshua hastily formulated a plan. "Lon and Joey, come with me. Wilko, take Katie, Wes and Ryan and escort the prisoner to the Hartfield and provide back up."

Questioning glances landed upon the XO, while the man himself met Rylie's wide-eyed stare.

His level gaze held the boy's. "Rylie, you said you know where they're keeping Captain Dave Mickleson. Can you lead us to him?"

"Yeah, it's an underground bunker. Charlie and I stumbled upon it yesterday." He looked pleased to be able to help, although edgy and likely anxious to have the ordeal over.

"Good. Wes, can I borrow your radio and headset?"

Wes removed the items and passed them to the XO. "Sure."

Graham Steele wordlessly grabbed the prisoner and thrust him forward. They fell in step behind Wilko as he nodded agreement and silently led his half of the group to the beach.

"Where's Ollie?"

Joshua talked softly into the radio transmitter, re-establishing communication with the captain, while Rylie answered Lon.

"He's okay, for now anyway. Charlie is looking after him. They're hiding in a cave beyond the river."

Lon looked puzzled. His expression begged the questions, why was he hiding and who was Charlie?

"He was shot when we were ambushed at the river," Joey explained, impatient to be on the move again. Like Lon, she too was worried about Ollie and wanted to get to him quickly. The sooner they recovered Dave Mickleson, the sooner

218

they could get medical assistance to their injured shipmate.

"Alright," Lieutenant Donnelly spoke in a decisive tone, "we have permission to retrieve Captain Mickleson. The last two pirates are accounted for. Farmer and his team intercepted one with a scar across his face swimming toward the pirate vessel after he tossed a grenade aboard the Hartfield. They have him bound and in custody.

"The second tried to start the pirate boat only to discover it had no fuel. Farmer and his men closed in to capture him, and seeing he had no way out, he detonated a grenade and blew himself and his boat up."

Joey cringed. "How awful! Did the blast injure any of Farmer's team?"

"Not that I know of." Joshua looked just as relieved as the faces around him. He quickly changed the subject. "Rylie, which way is it?"

The teenager frowned, slightly derailed by the news of the pirates' demise. "Which way is what?"

"The bunker?"

"Oh." He pointed off to their right. "It's not far, but be careful, it's booby-trapped."

Joshua glanced back at Lon and Joey. "Single file." He took the lead, placing himself between danger and the boy. He smiled. "Okay Rylie, give me fair warning before I stumble into anything nasty."

Rylie smiled in amusement. "Yes sir."

~

Wilko and his team arrived on the beach to find a RHIB melted and smoking at the water's edge. The second was nowhere to be seen, that was, until his gaze rested upon the pirates' ship in flames in the cove to the east.

The RHIB was floating a safe distance from the burning vessel, silhouetted against the raging fire consuming every last inch of the pirate craft. An orange glow lit the surrounding water and shoreline.

Ryan looked horrified, aware that a man had been on board when it exploded. Wes appeared elated that the victory was theirs.

Katie directed a smirk at their prisoner. "There goes your buddies and your only hope of escape."

Graham Steele smiled, also enjoying the thrill of payback and triumph. Wilko glanced at them both and then at the wreckage which was now beginning to sink. He felt no joy or sense of satisfaction as his comrades did.

His mind involuntarily played back a scene aboard the Hartfield of a small Asian woman facing an impenitent criminal and speaking words he was sure he would never forget.

"I have something I need to say to you," Joey had addressed the prisoner with her chin stubbornly jutted out.

"Get lost! I wish you'd drowned."

"That's just tough luck, isn't it." She had drawn a deep breath. *"I forgive you."*

Zacutti's bitter eyes had swung upward to meet hers. "I don't want your forgiveness!"

A mischievous little smile played about her lips. "Well you've got it whether you want it or not." With that, she had turned and calmly walked out.

Wilko shook his head even now. In that encounter she had shown love for her enemy and it had shaken his world to the core. His reaction would normally be that of Katie and Graham Steele's, triumph and revenge.

However this time something held him back. A challenge, issued by a God he had never met, and lived out by a woman who obviously followed Him. He could not define what it was he was feeling. Yet he knew that something inside him was longing, was searching, was changing.

29

Rylie put a hand on the lieutenant's arm. "This is the place. There's a trap door in the middle of that gully." He pointed down an embankment to a flat space of ground several metres wide and at least that many long.

Here the moonlight streamed freely through the gap in the canopy above, illuminating the area quite well. Joshua took a step forward and Rylie quickly grasped his arm and pulled him back.

"No, not that way. It's a rockslide. Go down from over there."

Joshua and Lon exchanged relieved glances and smiled.

"Glad we brought you along, kid." Lon tussled the teenager's hair and circled around to the right.

Joshua, Joey and Rylie followed. By unspoken agreement, Joey crouched low, hidden by the undergrowth on the edge of the clearing to wait with Rylie and provide cover for the men. Lon approached the centre of the clearing on stealthy feet, his rifle to his shoulder and his trained eyes scouring every tree, shrub and shadow. Joshua approached behind him, pistol in both hands aimed somewhere ahead of his feet. He turned in slow half circles to cover Lon's back.

Lon stumbled a moment when his foot caught on something solid. He stopped, knelt and felt around with his left hand. His fingers alighted on a steel handle hidden by a carpet of dead leaves and moss. Joshua noticed the focus of the bosun's attention and met his gaze when Lon glanced up.

With hand gestures, Joshua indicated for Lon to open the hatch while he peered inside. The bosun nodded silent agreement, waited for the count of three and lifted. They stood back for a moment, wary of the possibility someone inside might blindly fire upward.

"Let me out of here!" a distinctly Australian accent shouted in frustration from below.

"This is the Australian Navy. Who are you?" Joshua demanded in a tone only a fool would dare argue with, pistol barrel aimed at the manhole.

"Australian Navy? Please help me? My hands and feet are tied. They're gone but I don't know for how long." Fear edged the voice.

"Captain Mickleson, is that you?" Lon called down.

"Yes, yes it is. Please hurry?"

"I'll be right down." Joshua smiled at Lon with hopeful eyes. "Stay here." He quickly descended the steel ladder into the bunker.

He dropped to the floor which sounded like steel under his feet. The interior was dark save for moonlight pouring through the manhole and a small shaft of light deeper into the bunker. He presumed it was coming through an air vent probably hidden amidst the undergrowth above. His eyes slowly adjusted to the darkness and he spotted a dark shadow against the wall not far from the steel ladder.

Dave's desperate voice bounced off the steel walls. "Please, my hands and feet are tied behind my back."

Joshua knelt before him, observing that he was on his side and his hands and feet were indeed lashed together at the back with rope. He fumbled in the dark with the knot.

"It looks like they've dug out a pit and dropped in a shipping container."

"They said they were going after the navy on the island, guerrilla style. You've got to warn your people."

Joshua smiled and loosened the rope enough to slip Dave's hands out. He answered as he untangled the captive's feet. "No need for that. We caught the scoundrels."

"There are five of them."

"Not any more. Two are dead, one is injured and the other two are in our custody, soon to experience good old navy hospitality." Joshua grinned as he helped the man to his feet.

"Thank you." Dave sighed in relief as he rubbed his wrists where the rope had chafed his skin.

"Let's go." Joshua stood at the ladder and indicated for the captain to precede him. He smiled as he added a piece of information he knew the man would appreciate. "The sooner we get you on board the Hartfield, the sooner we can fetch your daughter."

"Charlotte? She's alive?"

Joshua could not see the man's eyes, but he would have to have been deaf to miss the sound of tears in his emotionally choked voice.

"Yes, Mr. Mickleson, she is alive and well, and even managed to help rescue one of my men."

The relieved father broke into uncontrollable sobs. Joshua hated to hurry him at a time like this, but Ollie's life was still in the balance.

"Please sir, we need to get back to the ship."

Still weeping with relief and thankfulness, Dave Mickleson climbed out of the bunker, his ordeal very near its end.

THIEF IN THE NIGHT

~

Leaves at the entrance to the cavern rustled unnaturally and deep masculine voices murmured to one another. Charlie's heart rate accelerated. She scrambled to her feet, collected a fist-sized rock from the floor and scurried to the entrance, crouching again and flattening herself against the wall.

She could hear someone crawling toward her and she raised the rock in her hand, ready to strike the intruder. The voices outside abruptly ceased. A hand appeared, then another.

She was a split second from bringing the rock down when a familiar voice called softly, "Charlie? You guys okay in there?"

She sighed with relief and tossed the rock aside as Rylie entered the cavern on all fours. The second he straightened, she grabbed him in a fierce bear hug.

"I heard explosions and gunfire in the distance. I thought you might be dead!"

Rylie laughed and squeezed her tightly.

She drew back to look at him. He did not appear to have any new cuts or bruises. "I even prayed to your God and asked Him to keep you safe. Are you okay?"

Rylie chuckled and glanced over at Ollie who was beginning to rouse from a fitful sleep. "Yeah, I'm fine. I've brought the cavalry. Ollie, it's time for us to get you out of here."

The sailor opened drowsy eyelids and blinked slowly. "Rylie?" His voice was gravelly from lack of use and most likely a great deal of pain. He managed a faint smile. "Good to see you're in one piece."

"Your mates are outside. The only problem is they can't fit through the entrance. Come to think of it, we had a little trouble fitting you in." Seeing no help for it, he looked to Charlie. "Come on, I'll take his shoulders and you take his legs. We have to get him out of here as gently as possible."

Charlie bit her lower lip. The move was going to cause some serious pain to the wounded man. "That won't be easy."

"Well, nothing we've been through up to this point has been easy so we should be getting used to it." He smiled dryly. "Sorry Ollie." He took the sailor under his arms.

Ollie leant forward to give Rylie better access to get a firm hold. He gritted his teeth to keep from screaming and allowed the two teenagers to squeeze him inch by inch out of the cavern. Several large pairs of hands were waiting on the other side and quickly took over when their injured comrade emerged.

Ollie's glazed eyes passed over each face illuminated by bright moonlight. "Hi fellas," he managed in a husky voice, too weak to so much as lift a hand in greeting. "Hey Woody."

Woody's gaze passed over his friend's bloodstained clothing and concern darkened his countenance. "I've got a few choice words for you, Ollie. Hiding out in a cave while the rest of us deal with pirates and hand grenades!"

He was lowered onto a stretcher and the medic wordlessly unwrapped the makeshift bandages to inspect the nasty wound, while Woody held the torch.

"The XO and Joey..." Ollie grimaced with pain as he gently felt the area for broken bones.

"They're fine," a mountain of a man assured calmly with a smile. "They're a bit scratched up but otherwise unharmed.

226

We brought in Dave Mickleson without a hassle."

Charlie stepped forward, eyes wide and full of hope. "You've got my dad? Is he alright?"

The huge sailor smiled at her.

"He's okay. He broke down when we told him you were alive and well. He's on board the Hartfield being plied with food and getting scrubbed up ready to see you."

Hot tears clouded Charlie's vision and she quickly blinked them away. She nodded thanks, unwilling to try voicing her thoughts for fear she would burst into tears. That simply would not do, especially in front of good-looking Aussie sailors.

She watched the medic fish a local anaesthetic from his kit and inject it carefully into Ollie's knee. He then offered his patient some strong painkillers. Ollie would need it all to survive the journey back to the ship. He re-wrapped the wound.

"Okay, I'm going to leave the dressings you kids applied, as well as the splint. You did a good job." A kind smile accompanied his praise.

Charlie and Rylie exchanged pleased glances. She was eager to reach the ship and have this ordeal over with once and for all.

"I'll be able to get a better look and clean it properly under florescent lighting with my equipment." The medic stood. "Alright seamen, lift him gently, and try not to jolt him. The bleeding has stopped and we don't want it starting again."

"Yes sir."

"How you holding up, Ollie?" The large sailor asked as he took the lead.

"Alright. It doesn't hurt much at the moment," the patient replied in a weary voice.

"That's the local anaesthetic. It's beginning to work."

Charlie and Rylie brought up the rear, excitement buoying their spirits and exhaustion weighing down their steps. It would not be long now.

30

Watching a tearful reunion between father and daughter, Rylie felt a pang of longing for his own parents. Would they be waiting on Pearl Island for his return? They would know by now that he was alive, thanks to the crew of the Hartfield.

Moments after boarding, he and the Micklesons were ushered below by a sailor who introduced herself as Katie. They were fed and then were able to recount their ordeal for the captain. Katie then showed them to separate quarters to shower and clean up.

~

It was all hands on deck when everyone was finally aboard. The dead pirate who had fallen in the pit had been retrieved and his body stored in the largest freezer aboard, which happened to be where the garbage was kept.

Wilko and Lon worked overtime with a team to patch up the ship enough to make it back to port. Yusef and Daz were posted on guard duty outside the auxiliary berth that now housed two captives, cuffed to their racks. Farmer and Jamie were busy tending to the burned pirate and to Ollie. Any other minor scrapes were being seen to by Joey, as she was the only one who could be spared.

Coz had taken over feeding the masses and Woody was

assisting him. Once the teenagers and Dave Mickleson were settled, Katie then joined Wilko and his team to help get the ship into shape. The captain continued taking statements and then buried himself in writing reports in his cabin.

Meanwhile the XO, Shep and Jaffa kept tabs on the bridge. In short, everyone was overworked and absolutely exhausted. Jubilant shouts broke out when finally the engines roared to life and the Hartfield began cruising for Crystal Bay on Pearl Island.

~

Joey cleaned up the clutter in the junior sailors' mess, which she had commandeered while the wardroom was in use. She had cleansed cuts and minor burns, some even recently incurred by members of Wilko's team, who were dealing with sharp steel that had been blown to pieces.

Her last patient had been Yusef, who had managed to escape guard duty long enough to allow her to remove a tiny piece of shrapnel that had lodged itself in his arm after a grenade explosion on the island. Up until then, in the press of demanding tasks, he had simply covered it with a bandaid.

Joey had carefully removed the small piece of metal, disinfected the cut and properly bandaged it. Thankfully it did not appear to need stitches.

In the mad rush since boarding the ship, she had managed only to briefly visit the head and quickly down a glass of water. No one waited presently at the door and she felt a glimmer of hope that finally she might be able to sneak off to the galley for a long overdue meal and perhaps offer some assistance there.

She used the sink to give her hands a wash with soap and water and felt a familiar twinge. She supposed she could not leave it alone for much longer. That submerged boulder had sure done a number on her left shoulder.

The river had washed most of the blood from the bullet abrasion above her ear, however judging by the stinging sensation in her shoulder, the gash was still open and oozing.

She was glad no one had noticed up till now, what with the chaos aboard ship it was the least of their worries. The last thing she wanted was to be a hassle when everyone was already stretched to the limit.

Joey unbuttoned her camouflage shirt and gingerly removed it, dropping it on the bench seat at the table. Beneath the shirt, she wore a standard issue grey t-shirt. She tried to glimpse the gash but simply could not crane her neck that far.

She carefully felt with her fingertips for the abrasion and found a large tear in her t-shirt. She winced with discomfort and withdrew her fingers. They were scarlet. She sighed.

She reached for some fresh alcohol swabs left on the table. "What a mess."

"I can see that," a familiar male voice spoke from the doorway behind her.

Joey spun in surprise. "Lieutenant Donnelly!"

He strode calmly into the room to stand before her. He spoke as he gently turned her around to inspect the gash. "Shep finally convinced me to have someone look at my back, which hurts like crazy by the way, and here I find the first aider in greater need of assistance."

She felt slightly embarrassed by his attention. "It's nothing really."

"Yeah right, Joey. This hole in your shoulder is still bleeding. How did you do it?"

She winced as he removed some material from the wound to get a better look. "I think you crashed into me in the river on your way past and then I collided with a boulder."

"That boulder certainly had a vendetta against you."

"Seems so." Joey turned around and had to look up to see his face.

His amazing blue eyes were somewhat distracting with that tender glow softening them. Joey mentally shook herself. This was the second in command!

Of all people to have romantic feelings for, I had to pick the XO!

She quickly looked away and took a seat on the cushioned bench. She leant her chin on her right palm, elbow resting on the tabletop. Joey was exhausted and really not up to dealing with emotional upheavals at the moment.

Joshua seemed to notice her fatigue and offered an understanding smile. He found a spare pair of latex gloves in the first aid kit on the table and put them on.

"Sorry, Joey, but you may have to remove your t-shirt so I can clean that gash."

Joey's gaze whipped up to meet his. The horror in her expression caused him to choke on a laugh.

"Not happening, sir!"

Joshua's eyes gleamed in amusement as he stared down at the tiny cook. "Then what do you suggest?"

Her dark half-moon eyes were wide with mortification. "Just cut away what you have to to get at it."

"Okay, but there will be no repairing the t-shirt."

She turned toward the table to allow him full access to her

shoulder. "It's kind of beyond that anyway."

"I suppose you're right," he murmured absently as he concentrated on cutting away a square of material with the scis-
sors from the first aid kit. He efficiently got to work cleansing
the wound, with only the occasional quick intake of breath
from Joey to indicate she was in discomfort.

He placed a waterproof dressing over the gash and then
tidied up the soiled swabs, dropping them into a plastic bag
at his feet. "That ought to do you for a day or so."

Joey turned on the bench, about to thank him and was
surprised when he crouched before her and gently moved
the loose wisps of hair near her left ear aside.

"I just want to take a look at your close brush with death,"
he said in a teasing tone, his concentration on the graze.

She was acutely aware of his nearness and judging by the
efficient, businesslike manner with which he cleaned the
graze, she was alone in that knowledge. She was disappointed and grateful at the same time. Romantic relationships
between crewmembers on board the same ship were strictly
prohibited, let alone one between a lowly able seaman and
the executive officer. It was unthinkable.

You've been at sea too long, Shafer!

And yet somehow she knew that what she was feeling was
more than a simple crush. Joey had admired the lieutenant from the first day he set foot aboard the Hartfield. His
humour, his fair dealings with the crew, his intelligence and
the care he showed for those around him. He had become
a friend, and now she felt the stirrings of something much
deeper.

You just had to didn't you!

"I just had to what?" He finished cleaning the graze and

looked at her curiously.

Joey's eyes widened in horror. "Did I say that out loud?"

Amusement now lurked behind those piercing blue eyes. "Yep."

"Oh... sir... I wasn't meaning you... I meant..." She growled under her breath with frustration.

Joshua chuckled and dropped the swab in his fingertips into a rubbish bag at his feet. He met her gaze, obviously unable to resist teasing her by waiting for an answer when she was clearly flustered.

"I was talking to myself. Growling actually." Her eyes locked with his and those tortured thoughts returned.

He looked long into her dark eyes, searching them, reading them. A smile played about his lips. "You just had to what?"

Momentarily she lost track of all reason.

Wow, your eyes are gorgeous! She was certain this time the thought remained internal.

Footsteps echoed down the narrow hallway, drawing their attention away from each other and back on task.

"That ought to do it," Joshua infused lightness into his tone. He stood and washed his hands at the sink.

Meanwhile Joey retrieved her shirt from the bench beside her. She had her right arm in just as Farmer entered the room. His eyes went from Joey's wincing face as she donned the other arm of her shirt, to the XO now drying his hands. He quickly deducted the circumstances.

Concern furrowed his brow. "Did you get hurt, Joey?"

"Just a small gash on my shoulder, which the XO kindly cleaned up for me just now." She was relieved to hear her voice sounding casual. However, internally she was scrambling for safe ground.

What if someone read how she truly felt about the lieutenant? It would be the end of her career, and possibly the death of his. Strangely, the thought of no longer being in the navy did not bother her overly much. However, someone questioning the XO's integrity and professionalism most certainly did!

Joshua's dry gaze landed on her. "It was a big gash."

"Does it need stitches?" Farmer drew closer, clearly wanting to inspect it for himself.

"I don't think it could have been stitched. The skin had been torn away. Take a look if you're worried," he urged the medic.

Joey held her hands up to both men. "I'm fine." She stood and continued buttoning her bedraggled shirt. "Now, if I'm no longer needed here, I'd like nothing better than to go have something to eat."

Joshua turned his attention to Farmer, knowing a losing battle when he spotted one. He propped his hands casually on his hips. "How's Ollie?"

"Stable. He lost a lot of blood which has made him weak. Other than managing the pain, there's nothing I can do for him. He'll need reconstructive surgery as soon as possible, maybe even a knee replacement."

Farmer's expression was grave. "The hospital on Pearl Island is good, but something tells me he'll need a chopper to one of the mainland hospitals for a job of this magnitude. Poor guy, he'll find himself behind a desk after an injury like this."

There was a heavy contemplative silence for several moments before Joshua spoke.

"And the burned pirate?"

"Lucky. We were able to remove the shrapnel which thankfully missed any major organs and arteries. The burns are bad though. We've got them cleaned as best we can, but he'll need ongoing treatment for quite a while."

Joey had always enjoyed nursing, just as much as she did cooking. "Do you need any help?"

Farmer smiled appreciatively. "No, we've pretty much got things covered at the moment. But thanks for offering."

"Then you may want to take a look at the lieutenant."

Farmer glanced at the invincible executive officer in surprise.

"He was shot in the back. The vest stopped the bullet of course, but I wouldn't be surprised if he has several cracked ribs."

Joshua looked at her through narrowed eyes. "Thanks, Joey."

He sounded anything but. Joey smiled haughtily and wandered from the room. As she departed she could hear the men talking.

"I'll need to take a look at that."

"I figured you might."

Joey smiled to herself. He was as bad as her when it came to receiving medical attention.

"Oh Joey." She sighed as she wandered down the empty corridor. "You just had to fall in love with him!"

31

The heavy wooden door to the enormous glass mansion was opened by a large man dressed in a black suit. Jack Coleman stood equally tall, although not as thickset, and stared past his hawkish nose at the intimidating fellow whom he supposed to be a butler.

The federal agent offered a polite smile. "I am here on police business to see Mr. Alexander Pritchard."

The butler's intelligent eyes clouded with questions. He opened the door for Jack and his partner to enter. Outside several more of his men waited, all on alert should things grow ugly.

The two men were led through a large foyer with a tall glass domed ceiling into a sprawling living room. It was furnished in a modern style in shades of red, with light coloured marble tiles and green potted plants against crisp white walls.

A sofa and two armchairs were positioned near large French double doors that overlooked a sandy white beach. There aqua water stretched to the horizon. Bobbing in the bay, tied to a long jetty near a small but luxurious yacht, was the federal police vessel.

Jack's gaze returned to the plush red lounge setting where a short, slightly overweight man in his sixties, was calmly awaiting his guests' arrival. He uncrossed his legs and stood, coming toward the two federal agents with a smile and an extended hand.

"Hello, I am Alexander-"

"Pritchard." Jack saw straight through the polite facade and offered no smile.

The silver-tongued gentleman shook each of their hands and gestured for them to take a seat. "And you are?" Alexander once again took his chair.

"Coleman," Jack began smoothly, "Jack Coleman, and this is Zack Turner. We're with the Australian Federal Police."

Alexander's brows knit with puzzlement and yet his cordial smile remained in place. "May I ask the reason for your unexpected visit?"

"We're here regarding your dealings with connections you made during your time as Foreign Minister."

"Yes." Alexander maintained an open expression. "How may I be of assistance?"

Jack's shrewd eyes lit with the delight of justice at work. "You may come with us, Mr. Pritchard. You are under arrest upon charges of drug smuggling, money laundering, kidnapping and blackmail."

In an instant those blue eyes regarding the federal agents grew cold and hard. "Those are atrocious accusations! You will understand that I will not be saying a word until I talk to my lawyer."

"I suspected as much," Jack answered calmly and stood, removing a set of handcuffs from his belt and approaching the suspect. "Zack will now read you your rights. Will you please stand and put your hands behind your back?"

Alexander complied, his icy glare boring first into Jack and then his partner as the cuffs where fastened around his wrists.

~

Lon emerged from the bathroom adjoining the room he shared with Wilko, towelling his short hair dry. His enormous frame made the ensuite look like a child's playhouse. The board shorts he intended to sleep in were bright orange, a stark contrast to the white walls of their berth. Lon tossed the towel in the laundry basket by the door. He dropped onto his rack with a groan and a deep sigh.

"I could sleep for a week!"

Wilko, who had already showered and was occupying the top bunk, was lost in thought and paid little attention. He finally worked up the courage to broach the subject on his mind.

"Lon, scuttlebutt says you're into religion."

"Nah mate, not religion. Jesus. I've enlisted with Him. He's my new Commanding Officer and my friend."

Wilko's brows shot upward. He hadn't expected that reply. "You talk like you know Him."

Lon stretched on his rack with his hands behind his head and grinned, eyes closed in contentment. "I do. You know, He's not like I expected."

Wilko scoffed. "You sound like some psycho nut just escaped from the loony bin." Even as he said the words, he knew they were not true.

Lon was as tough as they came. There was no one he would rather have backing him than the bosun. He was calm and rational in a crisis, courageous in battle and fair in his dealings with the men in his charge.

"Yeah, that's what I thought of Joey too when she talked

about it. But she was right, you can know God personally. I don't hear voices or anything like that, but I feel His presence and it gives me peace. I'm also happier than I've ever been, not because my circumstances have changed, but the emptiness inside me is filled. I guess I can't explain it any better than that."

Deep curiosity drove Wilko to search further. "What is it you both believe exactly? I mean, I know you believe in loving your enemies and forgiving and all that. I've seen Joey do it. I just don't get why."

Lon stared at the underside of the bunk above him contemplatively. "Well, I'm kind of new to this so I don't have all the answers," he began thoughtfully, "but it's got something to do with us being kind of like God's enemies."

Wilko was lost already. "How's that?"

"From what I gather, the bad stuff we humans do is against God's laws, making us like His enemies. But God isn't like us. He loves those who hate Him, and He sent His Son to die for those who pretty much stuck it in His face.

"You see, God has a death penalty for breaking His laws. I found that out the other day. Except He loves us humans so much He doesn't want to put us to death, so Jesus His Son paid the death penalty for us. But it's kind of like a gift, unless you take it in your hands and open it, you're still stuck on death row."

"So what Jesus did is kind of like a get-out-of-jail-free card?"

"Kind of, but better. It's personal. When you tell Him you're sorry for all the bad stuff you've done, and make that gift your own, then He comes into your life and becomes a friend and a commander all at once. Well, probably more like an

Admiral."

Wilko was satisfied with the explanation. The navy he could understand. Anything beyond that was a foreign language. "How do I talk to him? Do I have to be inside a church, or see a priest or what?"

Lon smiled broadly with delight at the simplicity of having a relationship with God. "Wilko, this is God we're talkin' about. You don't have to see a priest or be in a church. He reads your thoughts and hears your words. Well, at least it seems that way. I mean, I asked Him to take care of the XO and Joey and Ollie, and He did. He brought them all back alive, and after hearing their story, it's a miracle they're not all shot to pieces. I didn't say that request out loud, I only thought it."

Wilko was struggling to wrap his brain around the concept of talking to a powerful invisible being. "So if I think something to Him, He'll hear it?"

"Sure." Lon shrugged and his eyelids drooped wearily.

"But if He's God, what makes you so sure He wants to hear from me?"

Lon pondered that a moment before coming up with an answer that seemed logical. "He wouldn't want His Son dying for no reason. If you don't talk to Him, then all His efforts to get you out of death row will have been for nothing. He loves you." Lon rolled onto his side and got comfortable, sleep stealing slowly over him.

Wilko frowned in contemplation. He was uncomfortable with the word love. It wasn't something he had experienced, not from his father, nor indeed from any other member of his family. He had been raised to be a man, and men did not receive or express affection.

He thought of the strong bond of mateship he held with his shipmates and supposed that was actually what Lon was referring to. There was nothing he wouldn't do for his mates, including laying down his life. Now if that was how God felt toward him, then he could understand the Almighty's desire to talk.

God, Lon says you can hear my thoughts. Wilko felt unsure of what the protocol was when addressing Someone of supreme rank. *I'm hoping that's so. I just wanted to say thanks for taking my place on death row. Lon's right about us humans doing bad things. I've been hateful and full of revenge on more than one occasion.*

Joey recently showed me a better way. I don't know what all of Your laws are, but I'm willing to find out, and I ask Your forgiveness for the times I've broken them. I'd like to enlist with You, if You'll have me.

Wilko waited in the silence that followed, hearing the sound of booted feet and voices on the deck above him, and feeling the list of the ship as it sliced through swells on its way back to port.

Then it happened, quietly and without fanfare. He sensed it rather than actually feeling it upon his skin. A large, comforting hand rested upon his shoulder and a word resounded deep within his being.

Son.

He had never been called 'son' before, and certainly not with fatherly affection. In that moment he knew he was loved, and there was nothing unmanly about it. Forgiven, accepted, loved.

Wilko smiled, finally understanding what Lon had meant about personal relationship. If this was knowing God, then he would gladly serve under His command all the days of his life.

32

"Oh wow, would you look at that!" Charlie leaned over the front rail and pointed at a pod of dolphins racing the ship early the next morning.

Rylie did the same to get a better view and his eyes lit with elation. The pair watched six grey dolphins clear the water and dive back under, only to repeat the process over and over again at high speed.

Sunlight sparkled off their sleek backs as they leapt and plunged repeatedly, enjoying the thrill of the race. After five minutes, they veered off, getting down to the business of hunting. They disappeared as the ship neared the heads of Crystal Bay.

Rylie watched in anticipation as the cliffs grew closer. Jaffa had informed him before he went to bed the previous night that his parents would be waiting for him when the ship docked.

Part of him was excited and the other part felt sick to his stomach. He desperately wanted to return to normal life where he felt secure and loved. At the same time was the awful knowledge that his experience had changed him.

His talk with Joey over breakfast had helped. She had set aside her regular duties of serving the crew and shared with him her own personal ordeal, both when she was a teenager and her recent abduction. It was comforting to know some- one understood what he had been through and had suffered the same feelings of mistrust, hurt, anger and frustration. Yet she had come out on the other side able to forgive.

He supposed the healing process would take time. Joey had encouraged him to speak openly with those he trusted about what he had endured. Rylie didn't think he was ready for that just yet, but God understood. He felt a deeper bond with his heavenly Father, who knew exactly what he had undergone in every painful detail.

Joey had concluded the conversation in prayer, which had brought immense comfort to the hurting teenager. And finally she had handed him a slip of paper which was now in his pocket. It was her phone number should he ever need an understanding ear to listen. He smiled to himself. Joey Shafer was one remarkable woman.

"Rylie?"

Charlie's voice broke into his thoughts. He had forgotten she was standing beside him at the railing.

"Yeah?" He glanced sideways at her, curiosity gripping him when he noticed her uncertain expression. It was most unlike her to be tentative.

"Would you mind if I come visit you sometime?"

He smiled kindly. "I'd like that, but you do know that I live in Sydney?"

Charlie shrugged as if the distance from Cairns to Sydney was an afternoon stroll. "That's okay. I can sail down the coast with my dad and jump ship at Port Jackson. He stops there a lot to unload cargo and take on fuel. I'll just catch a plane home when you're sick of me."

Rylie marvelled at her independent spirit and smiled broadly. "Sounds like a plan to me."

She looked at him thoughtfully. "Hey, do you suppose I

could come with you to church when I visit?"

Rylie's grin was full blown. "I'll plan on it. When are you coming?"

They both laughed.

"Well, never if my dad has anything to say about it. He says he's not letting me set foot on another ship until I'm ninety. I'll talk him around." She smiled confidently and let her gaze wander to the cliffs on either side of the HMAS Hartfield as it cruised past into the bay.

Rylie chuckled and let his gaze wander as well. He had a sense that the trials they had shared had somehow knitted them together in a friendship that would last a lifetime. And if Charlie's interest in God was genuine, of which he was certain, then it would span eternity too.

~

Elizabeth and Ezekiel Hunter could scarcely keep still while the two patients were carried by stretcher off the Hartfield to waiting ambulances. Rylie waved to his mother who was already weeping. He then grinned at his father, who also looked overwhelmed. He had glistening rivulets streaming down his cheeks.

Rylie thanked the crew assembled on the quarter deck one more time, shook the captain's hand, and then tore down the gangway. He flung himself at his parents, who caught him in a group embrace and unashamedly praised God for his return.

Dave Mickleson stood on the quarter deck with an arm around his daughter's shoulders and they both grinned.

"Sorry to ruin the moment with business," Commander Kelly addressed his crew, "but the feds will be arriving any minute looking for their prisoners. Seaman Oldham, will you kindly relay my orders for Able Seaman Steele and Seaman Glover to bring the prisoners topside. Lieutenant Donnelly, will you please handle the transfer?"

"Yes sir."

Wes and Jamie left to carry out the order.

"As for everyone else, I'm granting you liberty until twenty-hundred hours. I want you all back on board sober and in your racks early. The basic parts we need to patch the vessel should arrive tomorrow morning from the mainland and I need you all on hand to get the job done. So until twenty-hundred hours, dismissed."

Commander Kelly saluted and the crew returned it, each face bearing either a restrained smile or a happy grin.

The moment the captain's hand dropped to his side, the crew scuttled in every which way. Most headed for the gangway. Coz was one of them. Seeing Joey hanging behind, he hesitated at the railing.

"We're going to see what's happening with Ollie. Are you coming with us?"

"I'll meet up with you guys later. I have something I need to see to first," she replied with an enigmatic smile.

Coz quirked his brows and shook his head, obviously wondering what could be more important than Ollie and liberty. "Suit yourself. We'll be at the hospital and then we'll probably head to the pub we visited on New Year's."

"Thanks." She lifted a hand in farewell and smiled as he

trotted after his shipmates. Joey watched the group wander up the pier and toward the town thriving on the shoreline.

The captain was conversing with Dave Mickleson and so Joey waited. In a moment they shook hands and parted, father and daughter traversing the gangway onto the dock. Joey approached the commander. Peace about her decision settled around her heart.

"Sir, I'd like to talk with you if you have time?"

The captain tilted his head to the side speculatively and studied her. "Sure Joey. Do you mind if we chat in the galley? I could do with a strong brew, especially when you tell me whatever it is that's on your mind."

Joey smiled in her easygoing manner. "That sounds like a good idea, sir. I've a hunch you're going to need it."

Commander Kelly chuckled and led the way below deck.

~

Joey joined her shipmates later that afternoon. Farmer had been correct in his prediction. Ollie had been flown immediately to mainland Australia by helicopter, where he would undergo reconstructive surgery. It was sobering news, however the crew gathered in the cosy bar not far from the beach, was celebrating a successful mission with no lives lost and all hostages returned safely.

They had visited Corey Knight in the Pearl Island hospital and were heartened that he would make a full recovery and would soon be transferred back to Cairns.

Coz and Farmer once again did battle at the pool table, while Katie and Switch took sides and offered helpful tips, much to their opponents' protests. Jaffa had finally managed an official sincere apology to Joey for the spiked drink on Lila Island. He was graciously forgiven and he celebrated by buying a round of beers, and for Joey a glass of non-alcoholic cider. The mood was light and playful.

Yet for Joey it was missing one thing. Joshua. She squelched the hope that had dared to flourish, took a small table in the corner, and ordered a meal.

Lon and Wilko came over to chat for a while, delighting her with yet more amazing news. The conversation was most unusual, a combination of Wilko sharing his story and both men asking questions about their newfound faith.

Commander Kelly and Lieutenant Donnelly arrived at the same time as Joey's meal. Lon and Wilko excused themselves to go have a beer with the captain, while surprisingly, Joshua dropped into the seat opposite her.

"That looks good. I could eat a horse." His eyes strayed to the waitress bustling between tables and the kitchen. He caught her attention and waved for service.

Joey wasn't quite sure what to make of his presence. "I don't think horse is on the menu."

True, they were off duty and allowed to socialise. Still, why had he sought her out, and in front of the crew no less?

Joshua smiled at her quip and spoke to the waitress as she came to their table. "I'd like what she's having." He indicated the seafood pasta on Joey's plate.

"Coming right up. Can I offer you a refreshment?"

"Just orange juice please."

"Sure." She jotted down the order and headed to the kitchen.

Joshua returned his attention to Joey. She caught his appreciative appraisal of her fitted soft blue shirt and denim knee length skirt. His eyes wandered to her long black hair falling freely around her face and shoulders.

For one moment under her unreadable scrutiny, he appeared to be intimidated. Joey had never seen him tongue tied until this moment. There was something behind those blue depths that he clearly wanted to say, but suddenly he seemed to lack courage.

She took pity on him and broke the ice, her eyes glittering mischievously. "I'm impressed."

"With what?"

"Mr. Indecisive didn't even ask for a menu."

He restrained a smile and leaned back in his chair. "I can be decisive when it counts."

She raised her brows in challenge, able to see straight through him. "Then maybe you'll tell me what's on your mind. I'm guessing you sought me out for a reason."

Joshua ran a nervous hand through his hair. Joey read his uneasiness and sat her knife and fork beside her plate, quickly becoming concerned. "Josh, what is it?"

"You're a direct person, Joey, so I'll just come straight out with it, okay?" He leaned his elbows on the table and opened his mouth to speak. Floundering for what to say, he closed it. He tried again and this time words came forth. "If I were to transfer to another ship, would you permit me to see you?"

Joey's eyes widened in astonishment. Was he asking what she thought he was asking? "In a romantic way?"

His uncertain gaze held hers. "Yes."

He was always so confident and ready to take command of any situation. And yet that request had cost him. She understood the difficult step he had taken in going out on a limb with the possibility of rejection staring him squarely in the face.

Joey's heart did a gleeful somersault. She hid her true feelings behind a poker face and shook her head. "No."

Although sadness entered his eyes, they remained tender with caring. "I understand."

Joey allowed a grin to peek through the facade. "I'm sure you don't."

He looked absolutely baffled and she laughed.

"I won't allow you to seek another posting just so that you can see me. I'm the one that's leaving. I've told the captain I won't be renewing my contract in the next couple of months. I'm planning on going into nursing.

"It's what I've always wanted to do since I was a child. Then when I was eighteen, well, you know what happened. I ended up here." She shrugged and smiled at him across table.

Joshua leaned back in his chair and a look of wonder came over his face. "Nursing. Good for you!"

"And good for you." She waggled her eyebrows mischievously and he quickly caught her meaning.

He grinned, showing a row of pearly white teeth. "So is that a yes?"

She deliberately broadened her Australian accent and winked playfully. "You can catch me, sailor, I ain't runnin'."

Joshua laughed and then determination laced his words. "I will, Joey Shafer. I most certainly will."

33

Deck hands, Jamie and Wes, looped large ropes over cleats as the HMAS Hartfield came alongside the naval base dock in Cairns. Other navy ships were moored nearby, both large and small.

Another Armidale class patrol boat, one of the four based in Cairns, was preparing to set sail. Crew were carrying aboard supplies not far from where the Hartfield now nudged the dock and came to a complete stop.

Six crews rotated through the four ships in the Ardent division, allowing maximum use of the ships and more days at sea. The multi-crewing system allowed two crews to have either leave, training time, or simply to be on standby to relieve another crew.

Normally the next crew would be ready to board the Hartfield, however thanks to a pirate grenade, extensive repairs were needed and would delay its next patrol. Wilko and his team had worked overtime to patch the ship at Crystal Bay enough for it to limp home to port in Cairns.

Now as the burble of the ship's engines ceased, Jamie wheeled the gangplank into place. Sailors dressed in civilian clothing grabbed duffle bags and filed off the ship, having well and truly earned their leave.

The captain would no doubt be bogged down in reports and meetings after such an eventful patrol, and Joey suspected that Joshua would probably be just as busy tying off loose ends.

Dressed in cut off jeans and a red t-shirt, she collected her bag from the dwindling pile on the quarter deck and smiled to herself. The XO was a man of his word. She had no doubt that she would hear from him soon.

She slung her bag over her shoulder and walked the gangway. Her feet touched the dock and she paused. Farmer had made her promise to visit the base hospital for a check-up, and to ease the nagging worry on his mind, she had agreed.

He had sent her blood samples for testing, however the results would not be in for at least another day or so. Joey was not worried. She knew what the drug was that Zacutti had used on her. He had used it the first time as well, and forensics had confirmed then that it was a herbal concoction native to the Pacific islands. In small doses it had no negative after effects. It was the after effects of her abductions that had a big impact.

She debated what to do and suddenly smiled. She would visit the chaplain and his wife and hopefully catch up over dinner. Joey navigated the busy pier and stepped off onto an asphalt parking area for sailors and their vehicles. Her old Land Rover was waiting faithfully where she had left it a week ago.

Just as she started the short walk to her vehicle, a black Mercedes was allowed entrance to the navy dock. It drove under the boom gate and past a guardhouse and two white uniformed navy guards. She studied it curiously, wondering if the admiral himself had come personally to see Commander Kelly and the Hartfield.

The fancy car cruised slowly into a car park several metres from where Joey was standing. The tinted windows allowed no view of whoever was inside. She was about to shrug it off, when a well-rounded woman in her late fifties stepped from the front passenger seat. Her richly coloured auburn hair was sprinkled lightly with grey around a softly lined face.

Joey blinked, hardly believing her eyes. The woman surveyed her surroundings with uncertainty until finally her gaze came to rest upon the small Asian-Australian sailor with a bag almost as big as she was slung over her shoulder. Their eyes locked and held. Time seemed to melt away.

"Mum," Joey whispered in disbelief. It had been four years, and yet her adoptive mother had not changed a bit.

Rebecca Hyndman's vision clouded with tears and her fingers covered her lips in an overwhelming mixture of astonishment and elation. A short, dignified looking gentleman in his early sixties closed the driver side door and circled the car to stand beside his wife. He glanced at her expression, which had eased into a huge smile, and his puzzled gaze followed her line of vision.

Walter Hyndman spotted his adopted daughter and froze. Joey watched as numerous emotions played across his weathered face. Guilt was the last to touch his features.

Joey dropped her bag and walked slowly toward her parents in somewhat of a daze. She stood in front of them for a long, silent moment, drinking in the wonder of their presence.

Finally Rebecca could resist the temptation to touch her daughter no longer and reached out a motherly hand to caress Joey's cheek. Joey felt tears sting the back of her eyes and quickly blinked them away.

"Wow I've missed you two!" She threw her arms around them both.

Walter's stiff posture relaxed and he hugged her fiercely in return.

"We missed you too," Rebecca said in an emotionally choked voice.

Joey laughed and squeezed harder. They finally stepped back to get a better view of one another, each face wreathed in a huge grin.

"How did you find me? I mean, how did you know the Hartfield was my ship and that it would be docking today?"

"We got a call from a federal policeman named Dylan Lawton. Admiral Broderick from Cairns had been in touch with him regarding two abductions. Officer Lawton made the connection between Jessica Hyndman and Joey Shafer and tracked us down to apprize us of the situation. Then the Admiral himself phoned several days later to let us know all was well and you were safe and would be docking this time today."

Walter's eyes were troubled, and Joey noted the weight of sadness in his countenance.

"Can you ever forgive me, Jess? I should never have sent you away."

Joey smiled warmly. "Dad, I firmly believe that all things work together for good. Wonderful things have happened as a result of my new life in the navy." She watched as a load of guilt lifted from his shoulders. Her eyes sparkled with a lively gleam. "Come to my place. I'm starved and I have so much to tell you!"

Her mother chuckled. "That's my Jessica alright."

She and her dad laughed, and the years slipped away.

EPILOGUE

Three years later:

Joey pulled into the naval personnel car park at the dock in Cairns, switched off the engine and awkwardly climbed from the vehicle. Her feet weren't on the ground ten seconds when she heard her name called from across the car park.

She glanced toward the dock and her eyes locked onto a tall, broad shouldered man with short brown hair. He was wearing khaki shorts and a light cotton chequered shirt. Her face lit with a smile of recognition.

"Ollie!"

She closed the car door and strode toward the pier. As she drew closer, his eyes dropped to her round stomach beneath a loose flowing shirt and his grin broadened.

"I've obviously been out of touch longer than I thought." He indicating her pregnant belly. "How long till there's a little Lieutenant Donnelly walking around?"

Joey chuckled and glanced up into his smiling grey eyes. "Two months, but it feels like it'll be two years at this rate." Her brows drew together curiously. "Hey, how about you? What have you been up to? We haven't heard from you since Josh and I married two years ago. He said you'd gotten out of the navy."

Ollie's smile faded and his expression grew serious. "Yeah,

after my knee injury I suffered a bit of depression. All I ever wanted to do was sail." He studied his feet. "Then I thought of you and all you'd been through." He glanced at her shyly. "I remembered the way you were able to accept your circumstances, forgive and then make the most of them. I told myself that if you could do it then so could I.

"I stuck at my desk job for another year, and as you know I saw you and the XO get married. But willpower wasn't enough." Ollie's gaze drifted out over the beautiful blue waters of the port. "That's when I bumped into the base chaplain. You know him. He explained to me how you were able to rise above your circumstances. At the time I didn't want to hear it. In fact, I got as far away as I could.

"I got an honourable discharge, travelled further down state and ended up working on a fishing charter out of Brisbane." Ollie chuckled and his eyes sparkled with humour. "But I learned the hard way that God never gives up. Turned out the bloke I was working for was a Christian just like you. Wasn't long before God caught up with me and I gave in the chase."

"Oh Ollie, that's wonderful news!"

"Tell me, how's the old crew going? I teed up with Woody to go diving over the weekend. We agreed to meet at the dock and hopefully grab a few of the guys and see if they wanted to catch up over dinner."

Joey smiled with delight. It was so wonderful to see him again, and better yet to see him so happy and healthy. "Dinner's a great idea!"

"Are you and the XO free?"

Joey grinned. "Count us in! I'm happy not to cook for the night."

"So, who's still on the team?"

Joey noted from the corner of her eye that the Hartfield was now slicing through the Harbour waters toward the dock.

"Most of the boys are still in Ardent one, although a few have been promoted and have taken on other postings. Josh still loves working on the patrol boat, as you've probably guessed. Wilko is doing great. We see him most weekends when he lands on our doorstep for a decent home cooked meal.

"Lon got himself married to a nice girl he met at church just last year. Coz was promoted to Able Seaman and is still in the kitchen. I guess you'll find out about the others in just a moment." She nodded toward the patrol boat that was pulling alongside the pier.

They started walking toward the ship in unspoken agreement.

"Hey, how did you go with university? You were studying to get a degree in something. What was it again?"

Joey smiled in her usual laid-back manner. "Nursing. I've just finished my final year of study. I figure with the baby on the way, my fourth year on the ward will have to be postponed for a while."

"Congrats." Ollie beamed down at her.

"Thanks. Hey, there's the guys." She pointed to the men moving around on the quarter deck in civilian clothing, most disembarking as soon as the gangway was set in place.

"Let's go say hi." Ollie strode toward the Hartfield with an easygoing smile.

The boys spotted him and soon he was swamped with solid handshakes, conversation and hearty claps on the back in greeting. Joey searched the deck but could not see her husband. However she did spot Coz as he disembarked.

He caught sight of her through the crowd of loud sailors all talking over the top of one another and made a beeline for her. With a huge cheeky grin, he grabbed her in a bear hug, ruffled her long hair and dropped a kiss on her cheek.

He indicated her round belly. "How's my nephew going?"

She jabbed him playfully in the ribs. "It could be a girl you know."

"You wouldn't do that to me." His eyes sparkled warmly and he draped a hand over her shoulder. "The world couldn't handle more than one Joey Donnelly." His eyes strayed to the men talking and laughing a few metres away and he frowned. "Hey, is that... Ollie!"

Coz moved toward the group. Realising he had abandoned Joey, he glanced over his shoulder. "Can you and the XO come to lunch with my family on Sunday? I forgot to mention it to the X today. It's my birthday and Mama says she's cooking up a feast. I told her I'd invite you both along. She's looking forward to catching up with you and so are my sisters."

"It sounds good Cozzi. Go say hi to Ollie." Joey knew how much they had all missed him.

Coz grinned and waved, turning his attention quickly to his former shipmate. His voice soon joined the loud chorus of fun loving banter. Joey smiled and shook her head. It was great to have them all together again, regardless of the noise.

"How's my favourite girl?" a familiar, warm voice spoke from behind her.

An excited smile lit Joey's face and she turned. She had not even seen him approach.

She reached up and around Joshua's neck. "Fine now."

He laughed and wrapped his arms around her expanded waistline, drawing her close for a tender kiss.

They drew apart. "Missed you."

"Yeah, I'm kind of used to having you around too." Her beaming face contradicted her casual words. "How was your patrol?"

Joshua picked up the bag he had dropped at his feet and slung it over his shoulder. He wore black board shorts and a rich blue t-shirt, bringing out the colour of his eyes all the more. He looked drop dead gorgeous.

But it was the lively sparkle in those eyes, and the kind character behind them that Joey loved the most. She marvelled for the millionth time that he was actually hers.

He dropped an arm around her and steered them toward the car park. "It was blissfully uneventful. How about you? What's been happening while I've been at sea?"

She thought to mention that they were going out for dinner with Ollie and the crew, but thought selfishly that a few minutes of catching up alone might be nice.

"Rylie called." Her eyes lit with pleasure.

After dropping the boy on Pearl Island, she had not heard from him for months. That was until one day he felt ready to talk about what had happened. At first their conversations had simply been about sharing, listening and offering encouragement and scriptural advice.

Rylie had called on several occasions later and ended up conversing with Joshua and the two hit it off. As healing gradually took part in the boy's life, their times on the telephone were filled with banter and good fellowship. He had visited on occasion and had over time become an extended family member.

"That's great!" Joshua smiled at her, looking pleased to hear her news and even more so to simply be in her company. "What's he been up to?"

"He's enrolled at Sydney University in some sort of computer course. That kid is way too smart! The stuff he can do on a computer is over my head. Anyway, he says Charlie has enrolled at the same campus and is moving interstate just so they can hang out."

Joshua grinned. "Are those two ever going to get serious with each other?"

Joey shrugged. "They're just good mates. Rylie says Charlie's a powerhouse. She's full of faith and is as confident and independent as ever."

Joshua chuckled. "That's great! Say, was that Ollie I saw back there?" He glanced over his shoulder at the bunch of sailors strolling down the dock roughly twenty metres behind them.

"Yeah, it was. He's got some good news for you too. By the way, we're having dinner with him and the boys tonight."

They drew to a halt, and turned and waited for the guys to catch up.

"Good plan, but after that you're all mine." His blue eyes gleamed with mischief as he looked down at her tucked snugly beneath his arm.

She squeezed him around his midsection. "I'll always be yours."

He grinned and dropped a kiss on her upturned nose. "You got that right, Joey Donnelly."

Dear Reader,

I have had a lot of fun writing this story and I hope you have enjoyed reading it too. Although I endeavoured to research and stay true to the Armidale patrol boat and life aboard ship in general, I hope the readers can forgive me for any errors regarding the everyday realities and protocol.

The characters, the setting and the plot are entirely fictitious, yet the moral themes underpinning this story are very real. Although I have not had to battle with circumstances as dire as Joey's, I have been challenged often to live Proverbs 31 and become a woman of valour, honour, strength and courage. I am still being challenged in this area daily.

Perhaps we will not all meet pirates or deal with a hateful kidnapper, or be faced by a raging river and perilous booby-traps, but we all face the challenges of life that can make us bitter or better.

I have discovered that it takes a courageous spirit to tackle life's daily trials and overcome, to forgive and not harbour resentment, to love in the face of resistance, and to humbly accept God's grace and help in time of need.

I pray that you will be inspired to be a person of virtue; full of valour, honour, strength and courage. But more than this, I pray that your relationship with God will be strengthened. When it all comes down to it, that is why we are here, to know and love Him.

If you've never begun a relationship with Jesus, it is my

fervent prayer that you will follow in the footsteps of those courageous characters in this book that faced their failings, asked His forgiveness, and began a lifelong journey side by side with Jesus. Believe me when I say there is nothing more important.

May God's loving fingerprints be all over your life.

To His Daughter.

P.S

I hope you will keep an eye on my website for new releases and other titles you may not have already read :-)

www.jayhdee.weebly.com